THE DANGER WITH DEMONS

The Elemental Witch Series: Book 3

TANIA HUTLEY

TRUDI JAYE

Chapter One

The world around me is muffled and indistinct, like I've been entombed in layers of bubble wrap or opaque wax.

I can't move.

As hard as I strain my senses, I can only make out vague blobs of color, and hear indistinct rumblings of sound. But even though they're unclear, each sight and sound is precious. I've been trying endlessly to figure them out and make sense of them, because without those small hints that the world around me still exists, I'd go mad.

Maybe I'm already mad.

I can't breathe. I can't scream. I can't smell anything.

The only thing I can do is think, and my thoughts are deafening. Overwhelming. Obsessive.

I have no idea how long I've been a stone statue, but I'm certain it's been several years. Maybe it's been decades, or even as long as a century since the Blood Council cast their spell and sentenced me to this existence. A half-life as a statue is eternal torture, worse than anything I could have imagined.

I wish they'd killed me instead.

Xander, Jess, and everyone I know must be dead by now. Whatever horrors Jeqabeel inflicted, it's long over. Did Baltimore burn, like I saw in the vision the Veritas shared with me? Did the people I love die screaming? Is there anything left on that other side of that opaque wall?

Wait.

I feel something.

Pain.

A burning sensation spreads over my limbs, and with it comes an unbearable exhaustion, as though every trace of life and energy is being drained from me.

As horrible as the feeling is, I welcome it with such relief, I'd sob with joy if I could. Something is *happening*, and even a painful death would be a million times better than the endless nothingness I've been forced to endure.

The pain in my lungs grows until I'm on fire, burning from the inside out. For the first time in forever, I need to breathe.

Somehow, I manage to suck in a little air. It feels like a thousand needles are puncturing my lungs. My mouth opens, but all sound is still locked inside me.

The vague, indistinct shapes that have taunted me all this time become more defined. I can blink, and when I do, the dark shapes swim more clearly into focus, looming next to me. Are they people?

My heart comes slowly to life, thumping painfully. I can move my hands. What's happening? Has it been so long since I became a statue that the council's spell is wearing off?

"Don't make a sound. They'll hear us," whispers a lisping voice.

It sounds like The Veritas.

But it can't be. After so many years, she can't still be alive.

I blink again, and make out the woman next to me. No, not a woman. A girl. Windows are high above us, letting in enough moonlight that I can see her features. Incredibly, she looks just like the Veritas I used to know. She has the same white hair and wide, anxious eyes. She's the same age, too, around thirteen, although she's wearing jeans and a dark T-shirt while the Veritas I knew had a thing for white dresses.

The other shapes around me are statues. Other witches turned to stone, their faces frozen into terrified expressions that send chills through me. I know exactly how they feel.

"Are you okay, Saffy?" whispers the Veritas. "Say something."

"How long?" I croak. It hurts to talk and I swallow hard, trying to force moisture into my dry throat.

"How long?" she repeats with a frown. Then she gets what I'm asking. "Oh, how long have you been a statue?" She hesitates. "It's been three weeks. I'm sorry it took so long."

Three weeks?

That's not possible. She must be lying.

But she's the same Veritas who made me into a statue, and she looks the same as the last time I saw her. Like she hasn't aged at all.

A rush of relief hits me, and I feel so dizzy I stagger. If it's only been three weeks, then the people I love might still be alive.

"Xander?" I demand, my voice still hoarse. "And Jess? Are they okay?" The last time I saw them, Jess had been tortured by the Unseen, and I used dark magic to save Xander who was all but dead.

She glances behind her, as though checking there's

nobody lurking there. "They're okay, but there's no time to tell you everything that's happened. We need to go quickly, before he discovers what I've done."

"Before who discovers what you've done? Magnus?"

She shakes her head. "Dallas is manipulating the Blood Council, and Magnus has become a figurehead. Tomorrow they're holding a ceremony to pass official control over to Dallas."

All of a sudden, the last meal I ate rises from my stomach. I lean to one side and throw up. I can't remember what the meal was, but it's been partly digested in my stomach for three weeks. The bitter taste burns my dry throat.

"Shhh!" The Veritas tugs my arm. "We don't have time for you to fall apart. We need to go."

I wipe my mouth on my sleeve. Even lifting my arm up that far is exhausting. I'm not sure I've ever felt so stiff and weary. "Wait," I croak. "The other statues. We have to free the other—"

"No time." The Veritas grabs my hand, forcing me to move, to take a step. She barely comes up to my shoulder, but she's strong and insistent. She pulls me along though my feet are clumsy and slow, dragging me away from the other statues, ignoring my protests. Now I know what those witches are going through, I can hardly bear to leave them in that state, but I don't have the strength to resist the Veritas. Right now a slight, thirteen-year-old girl is a lot stronger than I am.

She leads me down a dark corridor and opens a door. Inside are shelves filled with odd shaped rocks. It's some kind of storage closet.

"In here." She tugs me inside.

"Why? Shouldn't we be getting out of here?" The

room is small and when she shuts the door behind me, we're crammed up against each other.

The Veritas turns on a tiny flashlight, and I realize what the objects on the shelves are. They're pieces of statues that have been broken. My gut turns over and I clench my teeth against another wave of nausea.

"You need to help unbind me from the council," the Veritas says. "If I don't break my council link right away, they'll be able to track us."

"You can break the link?" I ask, wrenching my mind from the chunks of stone around us.

"Most can't. I can. But I need some of your magic to do it."

"But—?"

Heavy footsteps march past our door, and the Veritas puts her finger over her lips, her eyes wide. We both watch the door as the footsteps fade away.

"We don't have time for questions," whispers the Veritas. She props the flashlight on one of the shelves to illuminate the room, and pulls a ceremonial knife from the pocket of her jeans. I don't see her cut herself—she's too quick and practised—but I catch the metallic smell of blood. My dark magic wakens, drawn to the power emanating from the Veritas's wound. Fresh blood, newly spilled. The urge to reach out and take her blood overwhelms me, and I try to move backward. I can't go anywhere. The closet is too cramped.

I take a deep gulping breath. When she reaches for my hands, I pull them away.

"I can't touch the blood," I tell her.

"I cut my arm, so you won't touch it." She grabs my hands impatiently. "Open yourself up to me. To my power."

I feel her pulling on my magic, dragging it roughly out

of me. I grunt in pain, and her hands tighten around mine, like she thinks I might let go.

I couldn't let go if I wanted to. White strands of magic are snaking from her hands, wrapping around mine, holding me tight. The strands creep up my arms, then wind themselves around my body, binding me in a suffocating web.

Dragging in small desperate gasps of air, I concentrate on not freaking out. It feels like her strands of magic are smothering me.

My dark magic wells up, even stronger and more demanding. The wound on the Veritas's arm is all too tempting.

Then she traps my gaze with hers. Her eyes are the same all-white they were when she was transforming me into a statue. It's creepy, but then, my eyes went black when I used dark magic, so I'm in no position to criticize.

The flashlight gets dimmer while her eyes get brighter and brighter. I can't look away from them. The whiteness grows until it completely fills my vision.

Then a picture starts to form.

Baltimore is burning. Buildings are in flames, and black smoke is billowing into the sky.

It's the vision I saw before the Veritas turned me to stone, but this time Dallas is standing next to Jeqabeel.

Dallas is shirtless, with a huge, bloody symbol painted onto his chest. A symbol that gives me a horrible chill, and not just because the blood red markings stand out in intricate detail on Dallas's lily white skin. It's the symbol the Unseen carved into Xander's chest as part of the spell to free Jeqabeel from Xander's body.

The demon is in its physical form, solid and real. Its body stands upright like a person, but huge and hairy, towering over Dallas. Is over-sized arms end in wickedly clawed hands. It has a jackal's head, and its fur is clumped with blood.

"You served me well," the demon drawls, its tone smug. "I will reward you as I promised."

"Thank you, My Lord." Dallas bows his head. "It was an honor to be your vessel."

The image vanishes. I'm back in the broom closet holding hands with the Veritas. Her eyes are back to normal... except for her expression of naked fear. I sag against the broom closet's shelves, using them to keep me upright.

"Now do you see?' she whispers, still clutching my hands.

"Dallas was the demon's vessel?" I demand. "The demon was inside him?"

"The demon *is* inside him," she corrects. "That was a vision of the future. When you reversed the Unseen's spell and Jeqabeel fled, it found a home inside Dallas. But that will be temporary. With such a powerful host to help it, the demon can easily regain its own physical form."

"But you said Dallas was taking over the council..." My voice trails off and I swallow against a wave of panic. This is worse than I could have imagined.

She nods. "The demon will have full control of their power."

"Did you manage to break your council link?"

Looking down, she seems to realize she's still holding my hands, and lets them go. "I did."

"Then let's get out of here." I crack the door open to peek out. The hallway is dark and silent. Whoever walked past has gone.

"Dallas has spies everywhere," she whispers behind me. "He's manipulating the other council members. Controlling them through the council link."

"Where's Magnus?"

"He's in Dallas's thrall. And that's not all. Jess..." She hesitates, looking stricken.

"What?" My heart turns over. "What did he do to Jess?"

"Dallas forced Jess to join the Blood Council."

I feel the blood drain from my face. "Where is she? We have to rescue her."

"Dallas has her under tight security at the conservatory."

"With the plant witches?"

The Veritas nods.

I push the door all the way open, moving into the hallway as fast as my clumsy feet will carry me. "We need to rescue her. We'll go there now."

"Not a good idea. We can't afford to be captured. There's too much at stake."

"I can't abandon Jess." The words are barely out before I stumble over my own feet and barely catch myself from slamming head-first into a wall.

The Veritas gives me a pointed look. "You're too weak," she whispers. "You couldn't save a dying fly right now, let alone face a witch with the power of a demon."

As much as I hate to admit it, she has a point.

"So what are we going to do?" I hiss back.

Instead of answering, she grabs my hand to pull me down the hallway. I don't object. Getting out of here without being caught is definitely the first order of business. I just hope she has some kind of plan for what comes after.

Chapter Two

M
y body feels like I've just run a marathon, but it's only been a few minutes since we left the safety of the storage closet and my feet still aren't moving very quickly. The Veritas pulls me along the mansion's long corridors, urging me to go as fast as I can.

She reaches a large door and pulls a key from her pocket. When she pushes the door open, moonlight hits my eyes and I drag in a lungful of fresh air.

I follow the Veritas through the door, and down a set of stone steps. It's the back of the building and there are no grand columns here, just practical spaces for deliveries.

A Jeep is idling in the no parking zone. I don't recognize the car, but a familiar set of shoulders is attached to the man in the driver's seat. My heart leaps into my throat.

I pull open the car's passenger door and fall into it, so overjoyed to see Xander that my throat closes and tears prickle behind my eyes.

The Veritas climbs into the back seat. "Get us out of here, Xander. Quickly."

Instead, Xander reaches over the center console to

grab me in a tight hug. His expression is full of love and relief and his familiar scent is so good, it makes tears prick behind my eyes. I was afraid I'd never get to hug him again.

"I missed you," he says.

I bury my face in his shoulder, my heart aching and my throat so tight I can barely speak. "I missed you too," I try to say back, though my voice is muffled against his T-shirt.

"There's no time for that now." The Veritas jabs my arm with her finger. "We need to go."

Xander gently pulls away. Losing his embrace is like losing my life raft in the middle of choppy seas, but I manage to hold back my protests as he turns the ignition. I want to get out of here too.

Instead of burning out of the driveway like I want him to, he rolls off at a sedate pace, and I wipe my eyes and nose on my sleeve.

"Are you okay, Saff?" he demands. "I swear, if they hurt you…"

"It didn't hurt, exactly." Tears threaten to overwhelm me, and I have to stop and drag in a shaky breath. "It wasn't pleasant. But it's over now." There's no sense in telling him how bad it really was. We have other things to worry about now.

His jaw clenches. "I spent every day trying to find you, but until Rebecca turned up out of the blue and offered to bring me here, this place was hidden. A spell or something."

"Rebecca?"

"My real name is Rebecca," says the Veritas from the back seat.

I turn in my seat and look back at her, feeling dumb. I don't know why I'm surprised she has a real name. Her parents obviously didn't christen her the Veritas. That would practically be child abuse.

There's movement on the seat beside her and my eyes go to a small animal sitting on its haunches, staring at me.

"Is that Ratticus?" My voice rises. I can't believe the rat is here with them.

"I had to bring him," says Xander. "I couldn't find anyone to look after him. Seems nobody likes rats."

"*Ignorant idiots*," says Ratticus into my head. I jerk back, blinking. I'd forgotten about his new ability.

"Did you…?" I hesitate, looking at the others. Xander is concentrating on the road ahead, and the Veritas is craning her neck to stare back at the mansion. I'm pretty sure they didn't hear Ratticus speak.

"I think there's something wrong with that rat," Xander continues. "He's too smart. Like *person* smart. Your magic might have messed him up."

"*Compared to demon-dude, I'm a genius,*" mutters Ratticus.

"I like him," says the Veritas.

"*At least one of you has some sense.*" Ratticus puts his nose up, twitching his whiskers.

The Veritas offers her hand to Ratticus, and he runs up her arm and onto her shoulder, nestling into her hair. Her expression didn't change when Ratticus insulted Xander, which confirms my theory that I'm the only one who can hear him. Not that I want to mention his new ability to her or Xander. They'll either think I'm crazy, or want to know what the rat is saying. And he's not exactly in the running to win any awards for being charming.

Instead, I watch the mansion get smaller. In all my life, I've never been so glad to leave a building. But near the council chambers is Rawlings Conservatory, which means we're getting further away from Jess too.

"We have to get Jess out," I say.

Xander nods. "We will."

"The sooner the better," agrees Rebecca. "When you've got your strength back."

"First we need to get you somewhere safe, where you can rest." Xander reaches out to take my hand, and I squeeze his in return. My body still feels unbearably heavy and my head feels thick. You'd think that after three weeks standing motionless, I'd be well rested. But it's the opposite. I feel like most of the life has been sucked out of me.

"Where are we going?" I ask as he turns onto the expressway. "Not to my house?"

Xander glances over, his keen eyes assessing my condition. "Rebecca thinks Dallas will look for you, and it wouldn't be safe to go anywhere he knows. We're heading to an abandoned cottage in Bellevue Forest. It's part of an investigation that's still in progress, so no one's allowed there."

I blink at him. "An investigation? Does that mean you're a detective again?"

"Yeah, it was strange." He shrugs. "After you disappeared, I got a call asking why I hadn't been turning up to work. When I went in, it was like everything that happened had been wiped from everyone's memories. Like I'd never been kicked off the force or arrested. I wasn't a fugitive anymore."

"That was my spell, the one Therese performed." The Veritas sounds proud. "I wiped all the information about Sylvia's death, and everything that came after it."

"You did it?" He gives her a nod in the rear view mirror. "Well. Thanks."

It seems so long ago, the day that Aunt Therese and Magnus rescued me from the police cell, changing the memories of Xander's colleagues. So much has happened since then. "What else has been going on while I was frozen?" I ask.

"There's not much to tell," says Rebecca. "Dallas has been getting more powerful, and I've felt him trying to influence my mind using the council bond. He's succeeded in controlling most of the other council members, but my magic's too strong. After tomorrow's ceremony, I was afraid that would change and he'd be able to use my own magic against me."

Her voice is small, and when I glance back at her, she looks young and frightened.

"Thanks for releasing me," I tell her. "Don't worry, we'll figure out a way to stop Dallas."

She doesn't reply, and after a moment I turn back to the road in front of us. I'd like to comfort her, but I'm too exhausted to be able to think of what to say. It would probably help if the odds against us didn't seem so overwhelming.

Silence fills the car for a while, until Xander reaches over and turns on the radio. It's a classics station, and when the soothing tones of Frank Sinatra murmur through the speakers, he grins. "I didn't do that on purpose, I promise."

It's a sign of how tired I am that I don't so much as roll my eyes at him. Instead, I give him a small smile. The soft crooning drains away what's left of my strength, and my eyelids slowly close.

"Wake up, Saffy." A hand on my arm drags me back into consciousness, and I blink blearily at Xander, who's still driving.

"How long have I been asleep?" I ask, rubbing my eyes. The road we're driving on is narrow and dark, with large trees looming on either side. My neck has a painful crick in it, and my body is aching. I shift uncomfortably, trying to stretch my back.

"A couple of hours." Xander's navigating the twisting road with intense concentration. The headlights are on low and not giving us much visibility, and it feels like we're in the middle of nowhere. It's like that moment in a horror movie where you just know something scary is going to leap out in front of the car.

"Are we lost?" I ask. The road isn't well sealed, and I understand now why we're in a Jeep.

Xander shakes his head. "Nope. In fact we've arrived. It's just ahead."

"*About time*," grumbles Ratticus. "*I'm hungry.*"

Sure enough, around the next corner Xander slows down, then turns onto a narrow gravel track that's almost invisible. He bumps down the uneven track for a while, until I see a small cabin.

As we get close, the car's headlights pick up a tumbledown porch and crime scene tape across the front door. In front of the cabin is an expanse of overgrown grass. Trees hang low over the roof, adding to the forbidding feeling of darkness and neglect. The place looks like it's been abandoned and forgotten.

Xander draws the Jeep to a slow halt in front of the porch. Grabbing a flashlight, he gets out to pop the trunk. As I prise my stiff body out of the Jeep, Xander pulls out a duffel bag. The Veritas still has Ratticus on her shoulder, and she and I follow Xander up the rickety steps to the cottage's porch. He pulls away the yellow crime tape from across the door, sending spiders scuttling out of the way. Then he hands me the flashlight, pulls out some long thin tools, and uses them to pick the lock. I'm immediately interested, and lean over his arm to see what he's doing.

"I didn't know you could do that," I tell him.

As the lock clicks open, he glances over his shoulder at me. "I have many talents."

"I'm impressed."

He gives me a ghost of a smile, pushing the door open. "You're an easy date."

Immediately the smell hits me. Musty, old, and rotting.

But also, underneath it all... *blood*.

Lots and lots of blood.

My heartbeat kicks up a notch, and my dark magic surges. The blood isn't fresh, but it was spilled with pain and suffering, which makes it powerful.

All I need is to touch that blood, and my dark magic will wipe away my oppressive exhaustion as though it never existed. The dark magic will give me strength and power. It'll make me feel better than I ever have before.

Xander hits a switch and a central ceiling light flickers and comes on. It's a dim, weak light, but it reveals old couches arranged around a fireplace, with a kitchen against the far wall and a doorway at the far end that leads into a dark hallway.

"The cabin has solar power, and there should be a full charge in the battery. If it runs out, there's a generator."

"Someone died in here?" I try to sound casual, but I feel anything but.

Xander puts down the duffel bag he carried in with him, and crouches next to the fireplace to examine the kindling that's in the hearth. Presumably checking whether it's dry.

"It's an ongoing murder case," he says. "A difficult one. This place'll be held in limbo by the department for a long while yet."

Murder?

My dark magic thrums in response and I grit my teeth against a stab of longing. "Not an easy death, then?"

Xander glances back at me, and something he sees

makes him put down the kindling he's holding. "Are you okay? Is the murder going to be a problem for you?"

I shake my head, dragging in a deep breath. The blood is tugging at my senses, enticing me closer. I know exactly where the victim died, near the kitchen.

"It's not a problem," I force myself to take a step away from the blood, all too aware that the Veritas is staring at me, her expression wary. Ratticus is snuggled into her hair, but his whiskers are twitching and I swear he's staring at me too.

"The good thing about this place is that the owner ran his illegal operation from here, so he was paranoid about security," says Xander. "He's got a perimeter of cameras and motion sensor detectors set up so nobody can sneak up on the house. An alarm will go off if anyone gets close, and there's an escape route out the back."

"You think we'll need it?" I ask. "Surely Dallas can't find us here."

"Given time, he can use his air magic to find us," says Rebecca, her voice flat.

My feeling of safety disappears. "How long have we got?"

She shakes her head. "Not long. Without my power, the council is weakened. Dallas will want me back."

"*We could give her to him,*" suggests Ratticus. "*Make it easy on all of us.*"

"Watch what you're saying," I mutter in an undertone, glaring at the rat. Ratticus's nose twitches and I know he heard me.

Rebecca frowns at me, obviously confused. "I didn't say anything."

"Sorry." It's too hard to explain that I wasn't speaking to her, so I wave an apologetic hand and move away from Rebecca and the cowardly rat. But without meaning to,

I've stepped closer to where I can feel the blood staining the floor. It's distant and faded, like it's been washed clean a dozen times, but the blood has sunk deep into the wood, dripping through the boards and underneath the floor of the cottage.

Murder, pain, and a long, slow death. The old blood is rich with suffering.

Would it really be so bad if I used it to get my strength back?

Chapter Three

I shove my clenched fists into the pocket of my jeans and drag in a deep breath. I won't give in to my dark magic. I have to resist it.

"At least we'll be warned if anyone comes close during the night," says Xander, opening his duffel bag.

"In the morning, we'll go back for Jess," agrees Rebecca. "We can't let her be part of tomorrow's ceremony. Her magic will make Dallas too strong."

"I brought food," says Xander, pulling out some cans.

"*Finally,*" Ratticus sounds annoyed. "*What took him so long?*"

Xander puts the cans on the ground. "I also picked up some clothes and personal stuff from your place. Here, Saff." He holds out a toiletry bag, a pair of jeans, one of my favorite black Metallica hoodies, and a selection of underwear, like he didn't know which ones to choose. "I'll start a fire, then heat up some soup while you wash and change."

"Thanks," I say gratefully. I turn on the dim light that illuminates the short hallway, and find two bedrooms coming off it, as well as a bathroom. After a short, luke-warm shower in semi-darkness, my exhaustion lifts a little. When I come out in clean clothes, with my hair brushed and my teeth minty fresh, a fire is burning in the fireplace, and steaming bowls of food are waiting on the table.

Ratticus is on the hearth in front of the fire, devouring a pile of rat pellets. Xander even filled a little bowl with water for him. Looks like he thought of everything.

My stomach rumbles, and I join the others at the table to eat. The soup Xander heated up is perfect. Warm, tasty, and just what I needed to settle my stomach. But as soon as I've eaten, my exhaustion comes back, settling into my bones. I have to struggle to keep my eyes open, and Rebecca looks just as tired. I guess she would be, seeing as she's only thirteen and it's the middle of the night.

"You both look dead on your feet." Xander pushes his empty bowl away, obviously thinking the same thing I am.

Rebecca yawns, her eyes sunken and dark. "Releasing the spell that bound Saffy into stone, and then breaking my council link took all my strength. And I can't stop thinking about that vision. It was the most vivid I've had."

"Vision?" asks Xander. "What vision?"

"Dallas is the demon's vessel," I tell him. "Just like you were, only Dallas has embraced it. He's Team Demon now, pom-poms and all."

Xander shakes his head. "I never liked that guy."

"I'm glad the demon's not in you anymore," I tell him. "But I can't believe it managed to escape into a powerful witch who's about to become head of the Blood Council."

Rebecca leans forward, her pale face serious. "We can't let the ceremony take place. If we rescue Jess and release her bond, Dallas won't be able to use her power. It might slow him down."

"So we break into the conservatory and get her," agrees Xander.

He says it like it will be the easiest thing in the world, but he doesn't realize how smart the plant witches are. Some people would say cunning and Machiavellian. If they were going to be rude.

"It won't be that simple." Rebecca frowns. "I'm not sure how many witches are under Dallas' thrall."

"Dallas might guess that we'll try and save Jess," I say.

Rebecca shakes her head. "Hopefully he'll assume we won't be that foolish."

"We should be prepared for a trap," says Xander. "Just in case."

I blink at him. Xander hasn't got so much as a scrap of magic, yet he's willing to walk into a trap set by a powerful witch? "I think I should go in alone to get Jess," I say. "You two can watch the outside of the place and make sure—"

"No way." Xander reaches over to take my hand. "I'm going in with you."

"But you're a mundane. What are you going to do when they use magic on you? Ask them really nicely not to?"

"It's good that he's a mundane," says Rebecca in her small, lisping voice. "We can't trust any other witches, in case the demon has been able to take control of their minds."

"I agree with Saffy that you shouldn't come along tomorrow," Xander tells Rebecca. "I know you're brave, but you're young, and it's too dangerous—"

He falls silent as her eyes focus on his. The power in her stare makes the hairs rise on the back of my neck, and it's not even aimed at me.

Xander swallows. "Ah. Okay. We'll all go in then."

"*I'll wait in the car,*" says Ratticus in my head. "*Leave the food with me. And leave a window open, in case you all die. I'll need to be able to get out and find a new place to live."*

I manage to ignore the rat. Just. "Once we rescue Jess, what then?" I ask.

"How about we kill Dallas?" suggests Xander.

"That won't solve our demon problem," I tell him.

"But it would make me feel better." Xander gives me a twisted smile. "Did I mention I don't like that guy? And he tried to kill me, so it's only fair we return the favor."

Ratticus makes a snorting sound in my head. *"Demon dude thinks he's strong enough to kill a witch. That's cute."*

The Veritas stands up. "Let's talk about it after we've slept. Saffy and I are both drained and we'll need all our strength back for tomorrow."

She dumps her soup bowl in the sink, then heads to one of the bedrooms and shuts the door behind her.

Xander raises his eyebrows at me. "She looks young, but she sure doesn't act it. Not many kids her age talk like that."

I can't hold in a yawn. "She's never been a kid her age. Being a Veritas has seen to that."

"What does that mean, exactly? Being a Veritas?"

"Truth. Justice. They're supposed to be able to see into a person's soul and understand their nature." I don't mention that she's the one who turned me into a statue. I'm pretty sure Xander wouldn't be nearly as sympathetic toward her if he knew. Besides, she was the only council member who argued against Magnus's ruling. She was overruled and had to go along with his punishment, but I could tell she didn't want to do it. I'm not holding it against her.

"Are they always so young?" he asks.

"No. But their magic is rare. We don't have another

Veritas in the state, and I think there are only about three or four of them across the whole country."

"Is that why she's so valuable to Dallas?"

I nod, trying to stifle another yawn, and Xander gets up from the table. "You look like you're about to keel over. Let's find somewhere to sleep."

I stand up too. "'Night, Ratticus."

The rat lets out a sound like a long, disappointed sigh. *"Hope you're not expecting me to keep watch."*

Xander takes my hand and leads me down the hall into a bedroom where a large, musty-smelling bed beckons. I find a linen cupboard in the hallway, and some not-completely-disgusting sheets and blankets. After re-making the bed with the fresh linen, we both pull off our shoes and jeans, but leave T-shirts and underwear on.

The moment I lie down, another wave of exhaustion hits me. I want to stay awake, to tell Xander how much I missed him, but I don't know how long I can keep my eyes open.

Xander pulls me close to him, and I nestle against his chest, my leg tucked between his, fighting against the insistent pull of sleep.

"It feels good to be able to touch you again," he murmurs in my ear, his warm breath sending shivers along my skin.

"I wasn't sure we'd ever be together again," I mumble. "Thank you for coming to get me."

"I'm sorry it took so long." His hand strokes down my back and I love the way his fingers feel as they steal under my T-shirt to caress my bare skin. "I searched for you every day, scouring every inch of the park. I swear that damn mansion wasn't there. Not until Rebecca finally turned up, asking me to be the driver for her rescue mission. Then she led me straight to it." He pushes my T-shirt up a little

further, his fingers making gentle circles. "Waiting in the car while she went in alone, that was the hardest part. She wouldn't have it any other way, but it was the longest hour of my life."

The memory of being a statue rises sharply in my mind. Time was my torturer, stretching endlessly until I'd convinced myself Xander was dead.

I give an uncontrollable shiver, and he stills.

"What's wrong?" he demands.

"Nothing. I'm okay."

"Saffy, talk to me."

I'm too tired to explain, so I kiss him instead. His lips open against mine, and he kisses me back with such passion that the weight of exhaustion lifts a little. His mouth is both soft and fiercely demanding. His cheeks are rough and his hands cup my butt, pulling me tighter against him. I can feel his need for me.

I groan, wanting him just as much, but all too aware that I don't have the energy to see it through. My limbs are too heavy, and my head is stuffed with wool. I feel like sleep is a mugger sneaking up behind me, ready to knock me out.

Xander seems to sense how I'm feeling without me having to tell him. He pulls back a little. "This can wait," he whispers, his kisses turning gentle. "You need to sleep."

"You're a good person." I sigh. "You're a better person than anyone I've ever met."

He's strong and brave, and I feel safe in his arms. He's dedicated his life to protecting others. I wish I were more like him.

I don't want to have dark magic inside me, or be attracted to blood and pain. I need his light and strength to help me keep the darkness inside me from taking over. To keep from becoming a monster like the Unseen.

"Everything's going to be okay," he whispers, his lips against my forehead. "You saved me from the demon when everyone else thought it was impossible. Together, we can find a way to kill it."

I sigh, wanting to believe him. Even now I can still feel the spilled blood in the living room. It has its own energy that calls to me, beating in time with my heart.

"I'm not sure I can control my dark magic," I whisper, already half asleep.

Xander kisses my forehead. "You can. You've got the strongest will of anyone I know. And you'll have me to help you."

I wish I could be as sure about it as he sounds. But Aunt Therese said the Unseen used to be a good man, and he certainly wasn't when he died.

How am I supposed to save the world, when I don't even know if I can save myself?

Chapter Four

My seat belt feels too tight across my chest, like it's constricting my breathing. Trying to relax, I take another sip of my takeaway coffee and let the hot liquid slip down my throat. All my muscles are tense.

It's early, just after dawn. We're almost back to Druid Hill, and though we're not going to the council chambers, the nearer we get, the harder my heart pounds. The conservatory is too close to the council chambers for my liking.

Xander is at the wheel of the jeep, his attention focused on the busy expressway.

"So you think there's any chance we'll just be able to walk in and grab Jess?" I ask, looking over my shoulder at the Veritas in the back seat. She's dressed in jeans and a hoodie, which at first glance makes her look like a normal kid. Until you see her eyes, then she looks about a hundred years old.

"Calla's in charge there. She's on the Blood Council, and loyal to Dallas. Hopefully nobody will be around this early, but if she's there, we'll have to overpower her." Ratticus is in Rebecca's lap and she's absently stroking him while she talks. He seems to have taken a shine to her.

"I don't get it," says Xander. "I've been to the conservatory dozens of times. Why would they keep Jess in a public place?"

"It's like the library," I explain. "Underneath the public greenhouses are secret basement gardens."

"Basement gardens?" He frowns. "How does that work?"

"Magic, remember?" I waggle my fingers at him. "With their plant magic, they can grow anything, anywhere. No sunlight required."

"And you're sure they're keeping Jess down there?" he asks.

Rebecca nods. "I saw Jess when they bound her to the council. Then Calla took her. I'm certain she's at the conservatory."

"Was Jess okay?" I ask. "Last time I saw her she'd been tortured by the Unseen."

"They had to drag her into the council chambers. She was spitting mad, and cursing Magnus and Dallas. Fighting all the way."

"That sounds like Jess."

"So we're just going to walk in through the front door?" asks Xander.

"I don't have a better idea." I glance back at Rebecca. "Do you?"

She shakes her head. Black smudges around her eyes give them a hollowed out look, like she's barely slept.

"Are you okay?" I ask softly.

She hesitates for a moment, then gives a reluctant answer. "It's the visions. They've been keeping me awake."

"If we can weaken Jeqabeel, maybe they'll go away," I say.

She shrugs, looking away from me, out the window. I wish there were something else I could say.

"So we all go in, and somehow get into the secret basement and find Jess. We figure out a way to get her out, and then escape." Xander gives me a sideways look. "Not the best plan I've ever heard."

I shrug. "What could go wrong?"

He shoots me a humorless smile. Yeah, I didn't think it was funny either.

"*I doubt you'll make it out,*" says Ratticus in my head. "*So I've decided my next home will be with someone who doesn't wait so long between meals.*"

Xander turns into the park, and we drive down the tree lined road. It looks so peaceful and quiet here. It shouldn't fill my soul with fear.

"Are you ready?" asks Xander as the conservatory comes into view. Just ahead, the tall glass windows reflect the early morning sunlight.

"Absolutely," I lie, wiping my sweaty hands on the legs of my jeans.

Xander parks the car, and looks at me oddly when I get Ratticus's rat food out of the trunk and leave the rat munching it in the back seat. He hands out the baseball caps he brought with him, and Rebecca and I both tuck our long hair up into them.

I stick my hands into the pockets of my hoodie as we walk toward the building. It's a crisp, clear morning, and it's early enough that there aren't many other people around, just a couple of joggers and a guy walking his dog. The conservatory doesn't open until ten, and it's way too early for any of the staff to have arrived yet. All the doors are locked.

Instead of going to the main entrance, we head to the side door that leads to the North Pavilion. Xander gets his lock picking equipment out, and while he works at the lock I check furtively around, making sure the coast stays clear.

The door clicks open and Xander looks through to check there's nobody inside before holding it open for Rebecca and me. We keep our heads down in case there are security cameras, and make sure the baseball caps are shadowing our faces. I don't feel any wards, but this is the public area, and wards would be difficult to maintain with so many mundanes going in and out.

We pass through the door that leads into the Mediterranean House, and I glance around, appreciating the beauty of it. Plants fill every space and golden sunlight pours in through the high windows and glass roof. Water tinkles in the fountains, and the fresh, sweet aroma of flowers fills my lungs.

The three of us move quickly down the walkway until Rebecca stops in front of a giant palm tree with enormous fronds that look like they reach all the way to the high ceiling far above us. She puts her hand on the trunk and mutters something.

A portal appears. On the other side is a staircase. Only the first couple of steps are visible, the rest of it disappears into darkness. It reminds me of the Unseen's basement stairs, and a chill runs down my back.

She glances back at us, her face anxious. "Come on," she whispers.

Xander follows her, stepping through the portal like he's done it a hundred times. I follow more slowly, my fists clenched and my heart racing. I'm certain this is a trap.

Xander turns back to me. "You okay?" He reaches for my hand, winding his fingers with mine, and we creep down the stairs together.

At least these stairs don't smell like the ones that led to the Unseen's basement. Coming up from below are the smells of living greenery, fresh and earthy. When we get to the bottom, the opening closes behind us, leaving us in a dimly lit tunnel. The walls on either side are dark brown, and the floor is soft underfoot. The tunnel's been carved from dirt. We're surrounded by earth on all sides, and though any normal tunnel would crumble without extra support, this one is magically held in place.

Part of me feels comfortable here. My earth magic likes being enclosed inside the ground.

Xander keeps glancing behind us. "It's too quiet," he mutters.

I raise my eyebrows at him. "You want it to not be quiet?"

"It feels wrong. It's a trap, isn't it?"

I nod. "Definitely a trap."

Rebecca glances back at us. She doesn't say anything, but speeds up.

Just ahead, the tunnel opens into a cavernous room filled with greenery. We have to slow down as we go through the doorway because enormous plant tendrils curl all around us, so we have to duck through them and step over them. This room is also carved out of dirt, but it's wide and dizzyingly tall. Dim lights shine down from far above us, and the light looks green, probably because it's filtered through so many leaves.

The room is packed full of so many plants, it's hard to take them all in. They all seem to be the same variety, their leaves a vibrant green with a distinctive shape, like an oak tree's leaves. They're rustling, as though being moved by a breeze. Through the twisting, rustling mass of vines and branches, I catch sight of a huge central trunk in the middle of the room, wider than any trunk I've ever seen.

Could all the vines and tendrils and branches belong to just one giant plant?

"It's like walking into The Little Shop of Horrors," mutters Xander, stepping over a thick root.

I frown at him, not liking the reference. "The plant in that movie liked to eat people, remember? Let's not give this one any ideas."

He shoots me a sideways look. "I thought you didn't watch musicals."

"Not usually. But I told you how my father spelled our television so it only played reruns of eighties shows and movies? I saw the movie several times as a kid."

"I love that movie." He blinks, then widens his eyes. "Wait, did a miracle just happen? Don't tell me we actually have something in common? There can't be something we *both* like, can there?"

"I didn't say I liked it, I said I was forced to watch it. The only bit I liked was when the plant... well, you know." I pretend I'm biting off someone's limb, chewing with fake relish.

Xander pulls a face. "That's gross. Saffy—"

"Up there." Rebecca interrupts. She points to the top of the tall trunk, and Xander and I crane our necks to see what's caught her attention.

Near the top of the plant, at least two stories up, is a closed, red flower that's the size of a small car.

"That's where Jess is," says Rebecca. "Inside that flower."

My mouth drops open. I stare at Rebecca, then back up to the flower. It's the shape of a closed tulip, its giant petals pulled shut. "How do we get her out?" I ask.

Before Rebecca can answer, a cough comes from behind us. I spin around and see an older woman with short, dark hair and a solid frame, wearing a bright yellow shirt and brown trousers.

"Calla," breathes Rebecca.

The woman gives us a smile I don't like, and reaches out to touch one of the giant branches beside her.

Instantly, the plant comes to life. Thick vines whip out, wind around my ankles, and yank me into the air. I let out a loud yelp, flailing my arms as the plant lifts me. My base-ball cap flies off, and all my blood drains into my head.

Rebecca screams and Xander curses. As the plant hoists me higher, more vines wrap around me, pinning my arms to my sides. I catch a glimpse of Xander swinging upside down by his ankles, then I see Rebecca dangling beside him, wrapped in so many tendrils she looks like she's in a cocoon. I struggle, trying to free my arms, but the vines are too thick and wrapped too tightly. There's no way to get them off.

All three of us are utterly helpless.

Far below us, Calla looks up and smirks.

"Thank you for dropping in," she calls up to us. "Dallas will be very pleased to see you."

Chapter Five

The tree hoists us higher, and Rebecca swings close, her face barely visible amongst all the vines that are holding her tight.

"How are we going to get down?" she hisses at me.

"Use your magic, Saffy," calls Xander.

"I can't move, and I need blood." I brought a knife with me, but it's in my back pocket, and with my arms strapped so tightly, I can't reach it.

As I fight against the vines, trying to work my hand free, the plant lifts us all higher, closer to the huge flower. My frantic struggling stills as I realize its petals are opening. I'm high enough to glimpse a figure curled up inside the flower.

Jess.

My stomach lurches. She's curled around one of the flower's tall stamen, and she's not moving. Is she still alive?

When I'm directly above the flower, the vines release me, dumping me inside the bowl formed by its petals. I land on top of Jess, before rolling off onto a sticky cushion of pollen. Jess doesn't even grunt, though her skin's warmth tells me she's alive. She's unconscious, covered with the gluey pollen.

A moment later, Xander and Rebecca both land next to me. As I struggle to my feet, the petals close over our heads, leaving us in semi-darkness. The pollen is all over me, sticking to my clothes and hair. The too-sweet air is thick and hard to breathe.

"Jess!" I bend to shake her, but she's completely out.

Xander pulls himself up to standing, helping Rebecca up too. "Use your magic, Saffy. Get us out of here." His voice sounds weird. He's speaking too slowly, like the pollen is clinging to his words and holding them back.

My limbs go weak and I grab one of the tall stamen to keep from staggering. My vision is starting to blur.

"The pollen," gasps Rebecca. "It's knocking us out." She drops to her knees.

I grab my knife and slice the side of my hand, a cut that should be deep enough to bleed freely. But barely any blood oozes out, and it's as thick and sluggish as my thoughts. My magic doesn't surge. When I reach inside, it feels weak and resistant. Usually my magic explodes from my body, but the pollen must be doing something to hold it inside me.

My limbs give way and I fall. Xander tries to catch me but ends up falling with me. I land on Jess again, and though I manage to roll off her, the motion takes me away from Xander.

"Saffy." His voice is weak and strained. "I can't keep awake."

My own eyes are closing and my brain feels like it's coated in sticky pollen. My body feels impossibly heavy. It's like I'm being turned into a statue again.

The thought sends a cold jolt of panic through me, and I snap out of the fog for just long enough to do the only thing I can possibly do.

I grab the nearest limb in front of me, Jess's arm. And I plunge the knife into it.

She groans in her sleep, and the dark magic inside me surges. It's not as strong as it would be without the pollen, but it's powerful enough to use.

The power feels good.

I bring up a rune on each arm and they burn into my flesh, clearing some of the fuzziness from my thoughts. One rune glows bright red like new blood, the other the dark red of old blood. The dark rune holds my animal magic inside me, but through the bright rune I use my earth magic to feel down through the core of the plant, all the way down to its root system.

Most of the spells I absorbed from the Unseen's grimoires are brutal, meant for destruction, wounding, and causing pain. I use one of those spells to tear the earth away from the enormous plant, roughly dragging the soil from its roots.

The flower shudders violently, shaking us around. I slam into the petals, and someone—Rebecca—smacks hard into my torso. The knife slips from my fingers, but my magic keeps ruthlessly digging into the roots, savaging the plant.

Its petals abruptly open, and the flower spits us out. We're too high in the air, and my arms flail uselessly as we fall, the others tumbling with me like dead weights.

I bring up another rune and use what's left of my earth magic to gather an enormous mountain of loose dirt, piling it into a giant soft cushion. We still land hard, and dirt fills my face, leaving me coughing. But I struggle to my feet without too much pain, so at least I haven't

broken any bones. Rebecca groans, then splutters. Xander pulls his face out of the dirt, spitting out grime and shaking his head as though trying to clear it. Only Jess lies still.

Calla is nowhere to be seen. Maybe I buried her underneath the dirt mountain without realizing it. More likely, she went to fetch Dallas.

I'm thigh deep in loose dirt, and it's hard to move through, but I struggle over to Jess and pull her face clear of the soil, lifting her from what looks disturbingly like a shallow grave.

"Jess, are you okay? Wake up, Jess. Please, wake up."

Putting my hand on the deep wound I cut into her arm, I let her blood coat my palm. My dark magic flares back into life, sending sparks through my veins. I drag in a breath, revelling in the heady feeling of strength and power it gives me, before I focus my animal magic into Jess, funnelling some of that strength into her and healing her wound.

She gasps and opens her eyes. When I let her go, she sits up in the dirt. "Saffy? You're alive!" She grabs me in a hug. "I thought they'd either turned you into a statue, or killed you."

"We don't have time for a reunion." Rebecca's covered with grime, and she's struggling to pull herself out of the loose soil, let alone climb down from the dirt mountain I created. Her movements are still slow, and her lisping speech is slurred. "Dallas will be on his way here. Jess is still connected to the rest of the Blood Council, and he can probably tell she's awake. We need to leave."

Jess lets me go at once, and I don't blame her. If Dallas had imprisoned me inside a flower, I wouldn't be sticking around either. Not to mention that the giant plant seems agitated, and vines are whipping around while branches rustle backward and forward. It feels and sounds like the entire room is moving.

Xander struggles to his feet, trying to stand in the unstable dirt. He's obviously still weak from the effect of the pollen.

"Wait, I can help you." I reach out both blood covered hands, offering one to Rebecca and the other to Xander. "I can give you both strength."

Xander grabs my hand and I direct some of the magic's power into him. He draws in a sharp breath, straightening his back. "Wowsa," he murmurs. "If you could bottle that, you'd make a fortune."

Rebecca makes no move to take my other hand. Instead she stares at me with her mouth twisted in an expression of distaste.

"Your eyes are black." She shakes her head. "You used dark magic?"

The look on her face makes me falter. "I had to. It was the only way to get us out of there."

"The more you use it, the more it'll consume you."

As if I don't know that. The knowledge already dominates most of my waking thoughts, and a lot of my nightmares.

"If I hadn't used it, we'd all be fast asleep, waiting for Dallas. Didn't have much choice." I glare at her, daring her to contradict me.

"No point arguing about it now." Xander's voice is strong again, and his movements sure. He takes Rebecca's arm. "Let's get out of here before the plant decides to take another bite."

"Thanks for the rescue party." Jess is already clambering down the dirt mountain. "Dallas forced me to join the council. Any chance you can break the bond?" Her face shows she's as enthusiastic about being part of the council as I was.

"I think so." Rebecca slides down the mound of dirt, assisted by Xander. "I'll try as soon as we're out of here."

Vines whip in front and behind us, as though the plant is summoning its courage to attack. Together we battle our way through moving branches and writhing tendrils to the door, using our knifes to slash at any that get too close. Once we're out of the plant room and in the tunnel, we head back toward the way we came in, keeping pace with Xander, who's half-carrying Rebecca.

"There's no other way out?" he asks, his gaze moving up and over the earth surrounding us. "I don't like this tunnel."

I don't like it either. We can't see very far ahead, and it feels like Dallas is waiting around every corner.

"It's the only way out," says Rebecca.

"I'll check whether the coast is clear." Jess races up ahead to the next corner. She peeks around the edge, then jerks back. A howling wind gusts past her, whipping her hair around her head.

"Dallas is here," she calls back to us. "He's blocking the exit." She's gone pale, and her fists are clenched. Lines of strain are appearing in her face.

Rebecca and I exchange a glance, and I'm pretty sure the Veritas is thinking the same thing I am. Dallas is probably trying to use the Blood Council link against Jess. If we don't hurry, he might be able to gain control of her mind, like he's done to the other members of the council.

"Get back," I tell the others. "Go back way we came." Snatching my knife out of my pocket, I cut my finger. Then I push into the tunnel walls around me with my earth magic, careful and precise. If I do this wrong, we could all be buried. The wind builds, Dallas sending his magic toward us. But at the same time, I focus on the part of the tunnel where it bends, loosening the soil in the walls and ceiling.

A rumbling fills the tunnel, then earth starts falling.

As we all scramble backward, the tunnel collapses.

Chapter Six

E arth and debris are still sifting down over us, but the tunnel is completely blocked between us and Dallas, and holding steady where we are.

Only one small problem.

"What now?" Xander runs a frustrated hand through his hair, showering dirt onto his shoulders. "There's no other way out."

"It won't take Dallas long to get through the dirt to us," says Rebecca. "But we've bought ourselves a little time."

A little color has come back to Jess's cheeks. Whatever Dallas was doing to her through the council link, the cave in must have interrupted him.

"I'm not letting them knock me out like that again," Jess says. "They'll have to kill me first."

The Veritas catches my eye. She's chewing on her lip. We both know that with the demon inside him, Dallas is stronger than all of us put together, let alone if he has the rest of the council with him. We can't win a fight against them. The only way to survive this is to run.

I put my hand on the wall of the tunnel. "I can get us

out. But I'll have to use dark magic. My regular magic isn't strong enough."

Rebecca frowns. "If you keep using it—"

"If I don't, we're dead."

"You need someone else's blood to use it, right?" asks Xander. He pushes up his sleeve. "Here, take mine."

I swallow, hard. But there's no time to be squeamish or worry about the way my heart leaps with anticipation at the same time as my stomach turns over. I slice him quickly, keeping the cut as shallow as possible, hating to hurt him. But the rush of power that fills me still feels amazing, overriding my guilt for the way he hisses through his teeth.

Blood oozes from the wound, not enough to really satisfy my blood lust, but enough to re-energize my magic.

With my hand on the wall, breathing in the pungent scent of the earth all around us, I direct my magic into the soil.

A giant, twisting hole digs into the tunnel's dirt wall. I'm creating a hurricane made of dirt. I push more and more of my magic into the hole, carving deeper and deeper into the earth. Taking a step forward, and then another, I walk into the newly formed tunnel.

"Follow me, and stay close," I tell the others.

I can't look back and check they're behind me, because I'm too busy concentrating on the magic. Pushing more and more energy into my dirt hurricane, I keep walking forward, keep tunnelling into the earth. When we're far enough inside the wall, I let the tunnel close behind us, so we're enclosed inside a bubble.

Only then do I risk a glance behind me. Xander, Jess and Rebecca are at my heels, all of us inside the pocket I've created.

I keep the dirt hurricane moving, keep it digging

forward, and make sure the tunnel behind us seals shut to show no sign of where or how we escaped. Let Dallas try to figure it out.

My heart beats in time with the relentless rhythm of my dark magic as it flows from me into the earth. I try not to think about what might happen if I can't keep this up, and we get trapped deep within the earth, unable to go forward or back. I just have to focus on keeping the hurricane going, tunnelling forward at a steady pace.

But I'm getting tired, and the power I took from Xander is running dry. The air is starting to feel thicker, and harder to breathe. I stop pushing forward and the darkness presses in. The blood is pounding inside my head.

"Saffy, you can do this," says Xander from behind me. "Trust yourself." He puts one hand on my back. It's the softest of touches, but it gives me a boost of strength.

Dragging in a deep breath, I force the magic to keep flowing. The circular movement of the earth in front of us creates a cool wind that whips at my hair. Debris hits my arms and occasionally my face, making me blink.

One foot in front of the other, we keep moving forward into the wall of dirt. I'm all too aware of the weight of the earth on top of us, and how easily it could collapse and bury us. The soil smells pungent, and I can sense the crawling insects and earthworms around us.

My magic's weakening fast. It's time to start climbing for the surface, and I'll just have to hope we've tunnelled far enough from the conservatory that we don't walk straight into Dallas's arms.

It's harder to go up because the dirt rains down onto us more, instead of flickering out to the sides. I have to crawl upwards, and I can hear grunts of exertion from the others behind me. My dark magic is weakening by the second, and the weight of the earth I'm tunnelling into seems to get heavier and heavier.

My magic is faltering, and my body is starting to shut down. It takes a huge effort to lift my arms and keep moving forward.

"Are you okay?" Xander asks from behind me.

I clench my jaw. "Getting tired. I'm not sure I can—"

The earth shakes violently, like an earthquake has just hit. I stagger, losing my grip on the hurricane and letting it die. Huge clumps of soil pound down on us, and I barely manage to keep our earth bubble from collapsing completely.

"It's Dallas." Rebecca sounds scared. "He's using his air magic."

I swallow. He must have figured out how we escaped.

"Can you start tunnelling again?" Xander tucks his arm around my waist, supporting my weight and offering his wounded arm. "I'll give you all the help I can."

Putting my hand over his injury gives me a brief jolt of energy, but my magic still feels depleted.

The earth shakes again, and more dirt rains down on us. Jess lets out a yelp as a clump of earth hits her. Our bubble is shrinking.

There's movement behind me, and then Rebecca pushes her way through Xander to stand next to me. "You need to get us out of here." She claps her hand on my bare arm. Her skin is warm and sticky. Wet with liquid.

My dark magic reacts instantly. It's blood, but not just any blood. It's the Veritas's blood, rich with her magic, that she's just smeared onto my arm.

Though my dark magic surges again, it's still much weaker than it was. I just hope it's enough to get us out of here.

Pushing my hands into the dirt above me, I send a fresh

blast of magic into the earth. We must be close to the surface, because when the hurricane forms, the dirt feels looser. I press forward, ignoring the debris that rains into my face, fighting to carve out as much earth as I can before the magic runs out completely.

I catch a glimpse of light, and cry out with relief. Behind me, the others cheer, and I can hear just as much relief in their voices. When we break right through, the dirt sprays up into the air, like a dirt fountain. Though it must look weird to anyone passing by, I'm past caring. I just want to get out of here and breathe fresh air.

Xander starts digging the dirt around us with his hands, helping my magic set us free of the earth. Rebecca and Jess join in, all clawing at the dirt, digging us out.

One by one, we clamber out of the hole, helping each other onto solid ground. My limbs feel so weak, I can barely move. Xander lifts me, hoisting me into his arms like I weigh nothing, and I go limp against his broad chest.

Though it felt like I tunnelled for miles, the conservatory is still in sight. At least we've emerged on the same side as where we parked the Jeep.

"Come on," says Xander to the others. "We should run before Dallas realizes that we're out here." He doesn't put me down, but lopes with me in his arms, carrying me toward the car. My teeth clatter together as he jolts me back and forth. It's uncomfortable to stay the least.

"Put me down. I can walk." I struggle out of his grip and manage to hobble along without stumbling. I can't quite keep up with the others, though. Using so much magic has drained all my strength and it feels like I'm dragging my legs through quicksand.

But we did it. We're free, and we have Jess.

Xander wrenches open the car door and is helping the

others into the back seat when a shout behind us makes me turn.

Dallas is at the entrance to the conservatory, his white hair standing out like a beacon. I'm almost at the car, reaching for the handle, when a blast of air slams into me, catapulting me down the road. I tumble, my arms over my head, leaving skin behind on the asphalt.

When I slide to a halt, Rebecca is running toward me, her eyes white and her skin glowing. Tendrils of her white magic extend toward me, creating a barrier to protect us from Dallas's magic. The wind still buffets me, but I manage to struggle to my feet. Rebecca reaches me and grabs my hand. I feel her tug on my magic as she tries to draw from it, but there's nothing left to give her.

The wind strengthens, trying to lift us off our feet. Rebecca's tiny hand clutches mine, and we lean into the wind, forcing our way back to the car. My skin tingles all over as her magic wraps around me, protecting me, but we still have to fight for each step we take.

The raging storm howls so loudly, it's deafening. It lashes the tree branches overhead, and rips bushes from the ground, roots and all. But whatever Rebecca's doing means the wind isn't strong enough to keep us from reaching the car.

"*Stop dawdling and get me out of here.*" Ratticus's frightened voice in my head spurs me on.

I wrench open the car's passenger door, while Rebecca lets go of my hand to dive into the back seat. I'm barely in the car before Xander pulls away. Though it feels like the cyclone around us is about to pick up the car and fling it into the sky, the Veritas's magic is still holding it back. Still, we fishtail down the road, skidding and sliding while Xander wrestles for control of the wheel.

Ratticus squeaks in protest as he's thrown around the

back seat. I'm too busy clinging on to be able to help him, but the Veritas grabs him. Xander has his foot planted, and the further we get from Dallas, the less intense the storm, until finally, the wind dies completely.

"Everyone okay?" asks Xander, his shoulders sagging with visible relief. He checks the rear vision mirror to see the others nod.

"*They're sitting on my food,*" complains Ratticus.

I'm so exhausted, my brain feels fuzzy. The adrenaline that was keeping me going ebbs away quickly, and I feel like I'm about to fall down a long black hole into a deep sleep.

"At least we didn't die," I mumble.

"*Not yet,*" agrees Ratticus. "*But it's still early.*"

Chapter Seven

I wake up nestled against a warm body, with arms wrapped tightly around me. Opening my eyes, I gaze up at Xander's intent face. He's carrying me up the steps of the old cabin in the woods, our temporary sanctuary.

"Hey." My voice is croaky.

"You're awake. How are you feeling?"

"Weak. That spell drained me." I slide my arms around his neck. Maybe I should ask him to put me down, but my limbs still feel half dead, and my head is stuffed with cotton. Besides, I love being this close to him. When the demon was inside him I couldn't touch him at all. Being against his chest, enclosed in his arms, feels like the nicest kind of luxury.

"Are the others okay?" I ask.

"They're already inside, getting the fire started. Jess is a little groggy. We think they kept her unconscious for several days."

"Has Rebecca cut Jess's bond to the council?"

"Not yet. She said she needs your help, but you were so deeply asleep, we couldn't wake you."

I swallow. With Jess still bonded to the council, Dallas won't even need to use his air magic to find us.

Xander pushes the cabin door open with his hip, and carries me into the dim interior. The blood on the floor sends a rush of longing into my core. It calls to me even more strongly than it did before, stirring my depleted dark magic and injecting a flush of energy into my veins.

Jess is lying full-length on the couch, her hand over her eyes. Ratticus is ambling down the hallway, sniffing at the floor. Presumably following interesting scents.

Xander sets me down gently, easing me into the armchair next to the couch.

"How are you feeling?" I ask Jess.

She turns her face to me. She's pale, with dark rings around her eyes, and her long blonde hair is tangled. Like me, she's still covered with dirt. "My head's pounding. But at least I'm out of that place."

Rebecca emerges from the bathroom looking a lot cleaner than when we clambered out of the dirt. Her wet hair is wrapped in a towel and she's changed into fresh clothes.

She gives me a sideways look as she sits down. "You can't use your dark magic anymore, Saffy. No matter what."

"How can you say that?" Xander sits on the arm of my chair as though he wants to stay close to me. "She saved our lives."

I'm grateful for his support, but he doesn't realise how dangerous it is to use dark magic. Rebecca's right. The more I use it, the more I want to use it. My blood lust is growing.

Jess looks over at Rebecca. "You need to dig that Council bond out of me now."

"I'll need your help," Rebecca says to me. "Do you have the strength?"

I shake my head. "That tunnel used up everything I have. I feel empty."

"How long will it take you to recover?"

"I'm not sure. I haven't used dark magic enough to know how quickly I'll bounce back."

Her eyes narrow as though she suspects I'm lying, and I have to remind myself that she's just a kid and probably doesn't realize how obnoxious she's being.

"Where are your parents?" I ask, suddenly curious.

Rebecca blinks, obviously startled by the change of subject. "They live a few hours away," she says after a moment. "They're small town people and don't like Baltimore."

"Are they…?" I don't quite know how to phrase the question, but Rebecca seems to understand.

"Truth magic comes from a recessive gene, and the last Veritas in my family was my great grandmother. When they found out what type of power I had, my parents didn't know what to do. In the end, they gave me to the Blood Council to raise." She shrugs as if she doesn't care, but I see a flicker in her eyes before she looks away.

Xander's eyes widen and I can tell he's shocked. "How old were you?" he asks.

"Five."

The word is short, clipped. But it says a lot. What kind of parents would give their child away?

"I'm sorry," I tell her.

"I don't need your pity, I need your magic," she says. "If we don't break the council bond, Dallas will find us."

"What kind of magic do you have?" I ask Jess.

"I don't know." Jess frowns. "Turns out the Blood Council bound my power, just like they did to you. Only they did it when I was so small, I had no idea. They told me I didn't have any magic and I grew up thinking I must be some kind of freak."

I wince. That must have been hard. But Jess and I still have unresolved issues between us. "And the reason you moved in with me?" I ask. "Was it because Magnus asked you to spy on me?"

Her eyes soften. "After I was arrested for stripping cars, my father gave me an ultimatum. I could move in with you, or rot in jail. But I never spied on you, or told him anything. I'm your friend, Saffy. I never lied about that."

A band loosens from around my heart, and I offer her a smile. "I believe you."

"When council members started dying, it freed my magic," she says. "But I didn't know what was happening. I thought I was going crazy."

I remember when Xander and I went to pick her up and found her terrified and disorientated by the side of the road. My gaze goes to Rebecca and I glare, silently demanding she share whatever she knows.

Rebecca flushes. "You can jump through time," she says to Jess.

Jess sits up, her eyes widening. "What?"

"Wait a minute." Xander holds up one hand. "Are you saying Jess can time travel?"

Rebecca nods. "That kind of magic is even more rare than the magic I have. Your mother was the first time witch to be born in generations."

"My mother...?" All the blood has drained from Jess's face. She looks like she's seen a ghost.

"Your mother vanished, and Magnus believes she died in the Nowhere. That's why he insisted we bind your magic. He was afraid of the same thing happening to you."

"But he told me my mother died in a car accident."

Rebecca twists her hands in front of her, her expression guilty. "Your father came home one day when you were small, and found you crying and alone. He thinks your mother must have made a mistake with her magic that killed her."

"When I accidentally cut myself, I went to a terrible place," whispers Jess. "It's dark and freezing cold. The only sound is a wind that whistles through your *soul*. I know that doesn't make any sense, but it felt like that wind was sucking all life and hope right out of my body." She takes a deep gasping breath, like she's reliving an unseen horror. "There were creatures there. Monsters. I couldn't see them properly, because they were only shadows. But somehow I knew they were evil. That if one of them touched me, I'd be in that hell forever."

Rebecca frowns. "You must have been caught between the folds of time. That's the Nowhere."

"That's what happened to my mother?" Jess's voice cracks. She's sitting with her back stiff and erect, completely motionless, like she can't move until she hears the answer. "She got stuck in that nightmare place?"

"Nobody knows for sure." Rebecca looks down, picking at her jeans. It's clear she thinks that's exactly what happened.

Jess closes her eyes, swallowing hard. Her expression is stricken.

I pull my heavy limbs out of the armchair and sit beside her on the couch, putting my arm around her shoulders. She drops her head onto me, dragging in a shuddering breath.

"How did you get out of the Nowhere, Jess?" Xander's tone is gentle.

"I don't know," she mumbles, her voice muffled by my shoulder.

"If you got out when you had no idea what you were doing, surely someone with experience wouldn't have gotten stuck there."

I can tell Xander's goal is to make her feel better, but what he's saying does make sense.

I squeeze her shoulders. "He's right," I tell her. "Don't convince yourself that's what happened to your mother. It could have been something completely different."

Jess's eyes flick open and she lifts her head, frowning at Rebecca. "If I time travel when I bleed, why didn't it happen when the Unseen had me tied up in his basement and was cutting me?"

"Because his dark magic was feeding on your power." Rebecca settles on the floor in front of the fireplace. "He was using dark magic to suck out your power to use for his own evil purposes. And the reason Dallas kept you knocked out was that he didn't want you to use your magic to get away from him."

Jess shudders. "I'd rather be drugged in a flower than go back to the Nowhere."

"Dallas doesn't know that," says Rebecca.

"How do I stop myself from time travelling again?" Jess demands. "I can't go back to that soul-sucking place."

"Can you teach her how to use her magic?" I ask Rebecca. "So she doesn't end up in the Nowhere?"

Rebecca puts her hand out for Ratticus who's sniffing at her jeans, and picks him up. "I don't know much—"

"Tell me everything you do know." Jess's voice is suddenly rough and angry. "No more secrets."

Rebecca bites her bottom lip, which makes her look like the kid she is, and puts Ratticus on her shoulder. "Your ability allows you to fold time, to bring the present and the past close enough to step between them. Because you don't know how to focus your magic, you're getting caught in the fold."

"How do I focus it?"

"You have to know where and when you want to go. Hold a picture in your mind, the sharper the better, and concentrate on travelling into it."

"Like a memory?"

She nods. "The more recent the memory, the better. The fold won't be so big."

"And how do I get back?"

"When you jump back in time, you're still attached to the present, and it will pull you back if you let it. They say it's like being tugged by a giant elastic band. So coming back to your present time should be a lot easier than jumping into the past. Just let yourself leave the past and you should arrive back in the present."

It sounds airy fairy to me, and I can think of several ways it could go terribly wrong. No wonder time magic is dangerous.

Jess sits forward, pulling away from my arm. "What else?" she demands.

"That's it." Rebecca spreads her hands. "I'm sorry, Jess. That's everything I know about how to do it. The only other thing I was told is how dangerous it is to change anything in the past."

"Dangerous?"

"If you change the past, it could mess up the present. Badly."

Jess nods, her expression drawn. "And that's really all you know about it? I just think about a memory to get there, then think about here to come back?"

"That's how I was told it works."

She drags in a deep breath. "Then give me your knife so I can try it." Her jaw is set and her eyes are determined. "If the only way I can stay out of the Nowhere is by knowing how to use my magic, I need to learn."

Rebecca holds up both hands. "Wait. It's dangerous, remember? If you change anything—"

"I won't change anything. I just need to know I can control it."

"You're going to try it now?" I ask. "But you're still weak from being knocked out."

"You don't know what it's like, Saff." A muscle ticks in her jaw. "What if I accidentally time travel, and I get sucked back into the Nowhere and can't get out again? I can't take that chance. I have to master it, and there's only one way to learn how."

"I lost my knife in the conservatory," says Rebecca.

"I'll get one from the kitchen." Xander stands up. "But you need to eat before you try anything. Recover a little strength. There's plenty of soup left over from last night."

"*I'm hungry,*" agrees Ratticus. "*Feed me now.*"

I stagger out to the car on legs that still feel weak to retrieve Ratticus's pellets. When I come back in, Xander's heating up the soup and Jess has gone to wash up. I take my turn in the bathroom when she's finished, washing off the dirt from the conservatory. When we finally sit around the small dining table to eat, I can feel my strength slowly returning with every mouthful. I hadn't realized how hungry I was.

We've barely pushed away our empty bowls when Jess picks up a small, sharp kitchen knife. She holds it over her palm as though she's going to slash her hand wide open.

My dark magic leaps in anticipation.

"Wait," I blurt. "Not like that. You'll bleed too much." I

drag in a breath, trying to suppress the blood lust that's surging through me. "Prick the end of your finger with the tip of the knife. You don't want too much blood, just enough to get the magic working."

"Remember to concentrate on when you want to go," adds Rebecca. "It might be easier to think of a memory with strong emotions associated with it. But not too far back."

Jess nods. She looks every bit as tough and determined as usual, but her trembling hands give her away. She catches her breath, then slices the knife into her finger.

And *vanishes*.

I suck in a loud breath, and Xander and I stare at each other with wide eyes.

"Holy shit," he breathes. "Did that just happen?" He leans back in his chair, his eyes flicking around the room as though expecting her to jump out from a secret hiding place.

My mouth drops open. I've just remembered seeing her vanish once before. When the Unseen came to our house to threaten us, she launched herself at him and the two of them disappeared. I thought the Unseen had performed some dark spell to spirit her away, but it must have been Jess's magic all along.

"There she is!" Xander jumps up so fast he knocks over the chair he was sitting on.

Jess has reappeared in the middle of the room. Only now her hair is tangled and her face is filthy. She grunts, punching with her fists as if she's fighting invisible attackers. Her eyes are wide and wild.

"Jess!" I get to her a moment after Xander, and she almost catches me in the face with one fist.

Xander wraps his big arms around her. "It's okay, Jess. You're safe. It's me, Xander."

I grab one of her flailing hands, trying to keep her from pummelling Xander. Her skin is freezing cold, and I can smell something nasty, like sulphur.

I glance back at Rebecca, who's standing by the dining table with her fists clenched and her face pale. "What's wrong with her?" I hiss.

She shakes her head, looking helpless. "I don't know."

Slowly Jess calms down. Her arms stop swinging and she curls into Xander, sobbing loudly. He eases her onto the couch, making soothing sounds, and sits on one side with his arm around her. I sink down on her other side and rub her back.

"What happened?" I ask softly when her sobs fade, although I'm pretty sure I already know.

Jess shakes her head, her lips clamped together. She's trembling, and her skin still feels icy cold.

"Where you in the Nowhere?" asks Rebecca.

Ratticus sniffs her leg, his whiskers twitching. "*Smells bad,*" he announces.

"I won't go back there." Jess glares at Rebecca as though this is all her fault. "I won't use my magic again. We have to find a way to turn it off." She wipes her nose on her sleeve. "It was worse this time. Like the shadows were waiting for me."

"Did you hold a memory in your mind? Maybe you weren't concentrating—"

Jess lets out an angry hiss. "You don't understand. They wanted to *eat me alive*. To take my soul. I almost didn't make it out." She pulls away from me and Xander, getting up on shaky legs and striding over to Rebecca. "You have to bind my magic. Take it away from me again. I don't want it."

Chapter Eight

R ebecca shakes her head. "I can't do that."

"Can't? Or *won't?*"

Before Rebecca can answer, a high-pitched alarm sounds.

"That's the proximity alarm." Xander jumps up. "Someone's close."

I leap up too. "What do we do?"

"We leave. Quickly." Xander hustles us toward the door.

Jess and I go with him, but Rebecca breaks away. She dashes for the dining table and grabs the sharp kitchen knife, shoving it into her pocket before rushing out to the jeep with us. I climb in the back with Jess, while Rebecca takes the passenger seat, Ratticus curled into her shoulder.

Instead of driving toward the road, Xander bumps across the grass, heading around the back of the house. The ground is uneven, and I grab hold of the handle above the door. Next to me, Jess does the same.

Behind the cabin, a rough stone and dirt track leads upward into the mountains. The trees are tall and thick on either side of it. Xander steers the jeep up the track, into the wilderness.

"How do you know where this leads?" asks Jess.

"We mapped the whole place out when we investigated the owner's death. This track crests this section of the mountain and then curls back to the main road." Xander's voice is calm, as though he drives up vertical gravel roads every day.

Jess looks anxiously over her shoulder, through the back window, as if she's afraid of seeing Dallas right behind us.

"How far away from the house would they have been to trip the alarm?" I ask.

"We should have a five minute head start." Xander keeps his eyes on the rough terrain ahead of us. "We'll be well out of sight before they realize we've gone."

Rebecca looks at me. "We can't wait any longer for you to recover before we break the council bond. We have to do it now." She tugs the kitchen knife out of her pocket and offers it to Jess.

Jess jerks away from the knife and shakes her head violently. "I'm not cutting myself again. No way. Not until you bind my magic."

"I can't bind your magic, and I need you to release it so we can sever your bond to the council."

"Forget it. I'm not doing it."

Rebecca hesitates. "There might be a way we can control your magic and cut the bond." She glances at me. "If the three of us form a coven, we can do both at the same time."

"A coven?" I repeat. It's an old-fashioned term, rarely used by witches these days. "You mean connect to each other in a magical group? Like the Blood Council?" I ask.

She nods. "If we form a coven, I'll be able to draw on your power to help me control Jess's magic. I'll have the strength to keep her from time jumping, and break her connection to the council."

"What about my dark magic?"

She swallows. "I don't know, but I can't think of another way to do this. There's more at stake than just Dallas being able to track us. It was through the council bond that he was able to control Magnus and bring the other council members under his thrall. He'll try to do the same thing to Jess. While she has that bond, she'll never be safe. And neither will we."

Jess and I exchange a glance. I can see my uncertainty reflected in her eyes.

If we're joined in a coven, will Jess and Rebecca realise how seductive my dark magic is? How their blood calls to me?

"How do we form a coven?" asks Jess.

"The three of us need to combine our blood. But Saffy and I will go first, and when you cut yourself, Jess, the two of us will draw your power out at once, trapping your magic in our shared bond."

"If I touch your blood, my dark magic…" I trail off.

"I think I can control it." Rebecca sounds nervous, and not entirely sure. But what choice do we have?

A blast of air bursts through the trees, shoving us sideways and almost knocking the jeep off the road. The trees around us whip back and forth, branches raining down onto the jeep's roof. I clutch the back of Xander's seat, my heart thundering.

Ratticus lets out a squeak and runs down Rebecca's body, into the footwell and then under the seat. "*Make it stop*," he demands in my head.

As soon as the car straightens out, Rebecca turns so she's sitting backward in her seat and lifts the knife. "We have to do it now." She slices the fleshy part of both of her palms, and her blood rises on both hands.

My dark magic surges with it.

The blood calls to me. It's coppery scent fills my lungs, and I can taste it in the back of my throat. I want it.

Dimly I notice that Rebecca's eyes have turned pure white, then my hand extends toward her of its own accord, reaching for the blood without me controlling it.

Before I can touch her, Rebecca slashes my palm with the knife and grabs my hand in hers.

My dark magic roars out of me, jubilant to be free.

It slams into a solid white barrier.

The Veritas's magic. The white wall tightens around me, holding the magic inside me. Rebecca's power is stronger than I realised.

I meet her pure white gaze, shocked by the control she has over my dark magic. My power batters at the barrier she's erected, but it doesn't give way. Her magic holds mine captive, forcing it down. White strands of magic curl around our joined hands, twining over our skin, holding our grip together.

"Now Jess must join with us," Rebecca commands in her Veritas voice, full of authority.

A blast of air hits the Jeep, rocking it violently. I slam against the door, dragging the Veritas half out of her seat. But the magic twined around our hands keeps us tightly joined.

"Hang on." Xander's voice is grim as he fights with the steering wheel, keeping us on the track. His knuckles are white.

"Do it now, Jess," orders the Veritas. She lifts the knife in the hand that's not gripping mine. Blood is smeared all over her palm.

Suddenly I'm filled with doubt. Is this really the right

thing to do? Rebecca could be tricking me into giving her control of my magic. She could be working with Dallas.

I try to pull my fingers out of her grip, to free my hand from hers, but the white strands of magic hold me tight.

There's an explosion behind us, and a burst of bright light. The force of the blast hits us, and the Jeep is blown forward. Heat sears over my body. The jeep fishtails again, and Xander forces us back onto the road.

Ratticus squeals in my head as I jerk around to look out the back window. Far below us, the cottage is burning. Smoke fills the air.

"Shit." I turn back to the Veritas. "Did Dallas blow it up?"

She nods. "Him or one of the other council members. He has all their power now."

Our hands are still clutched together. Somehow her magic is still wrapped around my dark magic, holding it down and keeping it subdued.

"We must join as a coven, Jess." It's the Veritas's expression—eyes wide with fear, tense lines around her mouth—that probably convinces Jess.

She takes the knife and stares into the Veritas's eyes. "Ready?" At the Veritas's nod, she pricks her palm.

The Veritas grabs her hand, gripping it tightly.

Her magic slams into me like a physical blow. Beside me, Jess cries out, obviously feeling the same thing.

The Veritas's eyes glow brighter, her magic building. I reach out and take Jess's free hand with mine, joining the three of us.

The Jeep jolts over bumpy ground, but inside the Jeep it's like we're glued together, held in place by the force of the Veritas's power.

The feeling of being cemented to the other two becomes stronger and stronger. I can feel their hearts beating, the air flowing in and out of their lungs. I feel the great breadth of space and time that comes with Jess's power, and the heavy weight of truth and justice that comes from the Veritas's.

I moan. It's too much. With my own earth and animal magic already inside me, plus the dark magic I absorbed from the grimoires, I can't fit any more.

I try to pull away, to yank my hands out of theirs, but I can't. My whole body is expanding, but cracks are appearing where it's growing too fast. Painful, wide, gaping cracks that want nothing more than to break me apart.

Just when I think I can't take it any more, strands of white light glide over my body, filling the cracks in my magic, making me whole where I'd been broken.

It's soothing and calm. I open my eyes, and see two sets of eyes staring at me.

It's done. I know the three of us have formed a coven, because our hearts are beating in time.

And my magic is muted. It's not completely dormant, like when it was bound, but the Veritas is suppressing it. My first instinct is to resist and fight her control. But it's probably a good thing. Maybe with her taming the dark magic inside me, my horrible blood lust won't be so strong.

"Now to get Jess out of the council," says the Veritas. I feel her pull at my magic, using it to search inside Jess for the Blood Council bond.

Carefully she uses a combination of our three magics to untie the connection. I sense when the link is severed, and Jess slumps back in her seat like a weight has been lifted from her.

Another violent wind rushes up the mountain, bursting through the trees, trying to catch us. The raging power of Dallas's magic, even from this distance, sends a shiver across my skin.

Chapter Nine

"Is it done?" asks Xander. He turns the car onto the main road, heading away from the cabin, and floors the accelerator.

Rebecca nods. Jess and I exchange a glance, and I know she's feeling as weird about our new coven link as I am.

My heart is beating in time with the others. At least, it feels like I can sense their heartbeats, and my own heart has joined in with their shared rhythm.

At least I can't read their thoughts. Hopefully that means they can't read mine. But we're connected, and it's a weird feeling. We're joined by strands of magic that feel like they reach right inside me.

"Anyone got an idea about where we can go?" asks Xander. "We need somewhere they won't think to look for us. Somewhere unconnected to any of us. And I don't know of any more inactive crime scenes."

"A hotel?" I suggest.

"Maybe." He shoots me a sideways look. "It's an option. But if I were searching for us, I'd make sure to check hotels. If we can find someone to stay with, we'll be harder to find."

"The only people I know are other council members." Rebecca sounds a little sad about that fact.

Jess leans forward. "I have a place, I think. She doesn't like phones, so we'll have to just turn up and see if she's at home."

"Who is it?" Xander asks.

Jess chews on her lip, an uncharacteristically hesitant look on her face. "She's a musician. A friend from a long time ago. I don't see her that much any more, but she's laid back enough that she probably won't mind if I turn up with three friends asking for a place to stay."

"Worth a try," I say, and Rebecca nods her agreement.

Jess gives Xander directions, then slumps back in the seat and stares out of the side window. Xander is intent on the road, though he's slowed down to the speed limit now that we've left Dallas and his air magic behind. Ratticus is back on Rebecca's shoulder, and she's turned to the front so I can't see her face.

Closing my eyes, I feel along the strands of magic that join me to Jess, testing our connection.

I can feel Jess's power. It's warm and bright, like sunshine. The exact opposite of the darkness that now inhabits me.

Turning my face to Rebecca, I feel for her power next. It's bright white, and almost painful to sense. It feels jagged and sharp. Is that what it's like for Rebecca when she uses it? Does it hurt?

All at once, I feel her power tighten around my magic, and a sharp pain stabs into my skull. I wince, flicking open my eyes to find her staring back at me from the front seat. Her eyes aren't pure white, but they're paler than normal, and she doesn't look happy.

"I was just testing our bond," I tell her.

"Well, don't." She turns her back on me, the discussion clearly over.

I meet Xander's gaze in the rear vision mirror, and he raises his eyebrows at me. I shake my head to tell him I can't explain what just happened and he gives me a small nod in return.

That's Xander. He's not pushy or needy. He's accepted everything without question. Magic. Demons. My new thirst for blood. I've put him in terrible danger, and it's a miracle he's still alive. Still, every single thing he does is to protect me.

I keep hold of his gaze and give him a small smile, wishing we were alone so I could tell him how grateful I am. Or even better, wishing I could show him. The night we spent together in Sylvia's athenaeum is still fresh in my mind, one of my all-time favorite memories. Which is a miracle considering the mortal danger we were in at the time.

What wouldn't I give to have all this over, and be able to just spend a night relaxing on the couch with him, watching bad eighties re-runs on my Dad's magic television?

He holds my eyes for a long time, as though he knows exactly what I'm thinking and he's wishing the same thing. Then his gaze goes back to the road, and his attention goes back to driving.

Now we're on the freeway, the road is long and smooth, and the car is warm. My eyes start drooping, and I'm almost asleep when I realise my tiredness is coming from somewhere else. Somewhere external to me.

In the front seat, the Veritas has fallen asleep. I can feel her heartbeats slow down. She lets out a low moan and

shakes her head from side to side. "No," she mutters. "No."

I exchange a glance with Xander, then lean between the two front seats to put my hand on her arm. "Rebecca. Wake up. You're having a bad dream."

She doesn't react, but I can feel her trembling.

"Wake up." I shake her, and she moans again.

Xander frowns. "Why won't she wake? Could Dallas be doing something to her?"

"I don't know." I glance at Jess. "Can you feel anything along our link?"

Jess is leaning forward, looking alarmed. She shakes her head. "Nothing."

"I'll bite her." Ratticus sounds way more enthusiastic about the idea than he needs to be. He nips her ear, but Rebecca doesn't so much as flinch.

"What shall we do?" asks Jess.

Before anyone can answer, Rebecca turns her head toward me and opens her eyes. They're the full white they go when she's using her Veritas powers. I have no idea whether she can even see when they're like this. Staring into them gives me chills.

She reaches out and grabs my arm, her nails digging into my skin. She opens her mouth, her expression intent, like she's going to say something really important.

Instead, she takes a breath and screams into my face.

I jerk backward, shocked.

Ratticus lets out a frightened squeak and jumps off her shoulder, catapulting himself at me. He lands on my arm and races up to my shoulder, leaving scratches the whole way, and curls into my neck.

"Rebecca!" shouts Xander. "Wake up!"

She blinks, then her irises start to become visible in the

whites of her eyes, like the picture appearing when an old television is turned on. She drags in a deep breath.

"Are you okay?" I ask.

"I… yes. I'm okay." She rubs a hand over her face. "Just another vision."

"It must have been a bad one. What was it?"

She drops her hand. Her expression is worried, but she doesn't answer. Her heart is beating too fast, and mine is matching it beat for beat.

"What was the vision about?" Jess leans forward.

"Nothing." Rebecca shakes her head. "It was nothing."

"Tell us," says Xander.

Jess nods. "However bad it was, we need to know."

"It was just a repeat of what I've already seen. Nothing new."

"So getting Jess away from Dallas didn't improve the situation?" I ask. "The demon apocalypse is still coming?" Though I'd known saving Jess wouldn't slow the demon's plans, somewhere deep inside, I'd still nursed a kernel of hope.

When Rebecca looks at me, something flashes in her eyes. "No."

She's lying. She's hiding something from us, and the only reason I can think of for her to do that is if the future she saw in the vision is even worse than it was before.

"What is it?" I demand. "What did you see?"

"It's the same as last time," Rebecca insists, but her gaze drops.

"Whatever it is, you need to tell us," I say. "We're a team. A coven. We all need to be on the same side."

I push my magic along our coven link, trying to feel past her barrier, seeing if I can sense her emotions. Instantly, her white hot magic blocks me, shoving my power back hard and fast.

Rebecca glares at me. "Is that what being a team means? Trying to force your way inside my head?"

"Then tell us what we're up against."

"There's nothing to tell."

I lean back in the seat with a harrumph of air. Rebecca turns back to the window. Xander shoots me a worried look in the rear vision mirror, but Jess gives me a shrug.

"Turn off the expressway at the next exit," she tells Xander.

She directs him to a part of town I haven't spent much time in. An older neighbourhood on the outskirts of the city. We stop outside a house with flaking paint and long grass outside, in a similar state of disrepair as most of the others on the street. The main thing it has going for it is that it's far away from Druid Hill.

I get out of the car with Ratticus still curled on my shoulder, and we all follow Jess up to the front door. When she knocks, it opens just a crack, and a pair of suspicious, dark-rimmed eyes peer out.

"Hey Morgan," says Jess. "It's me. I brought some friends over."

The door opens wider. "Jess! Oh man, I thought you were the landlord looking for his rent." The woman motions Jess inside before dragging her into a quick hug. She has a scratchy, hoarse voice, like she smokes ten packs a day. Her long hair is dyed black with bright purple highlights, and she's wearing layers of black clothing and thick makeup. If she's in a band, I'm guessing it's goth metal.

"These are my friends, Saffy, Rebecca, and Xander." Jess motions to us and we follow her inside. Morgan greets us with, "Hey," and a friendly wave, seemingly unconcerned that Jess has turned up with a group of people she doesn't know.

"You just caught me, Jess." She leads us into a living room. "Half an hour and I would have been gone."

Inside the house there's band equipment everywhere, a drum set stacked in one corner of the living room, guitar cases in another corner. Leads and amps and power outlets drip over everything, including the furniture, making it difficult to walk far. There's a big stereo against the wall, and it's playing weird sonorous music that could possibly be whale song, or a woman moaning in pain. I'm not really sure.

"I wish this was just a social call." Jess sounds apologetic. "I know we haven't caught up in ages. But the truth is, we need somewhere to hide out."

"Oh man, in trouble with the cops? That's a bummer." She looks sympathetic, beaming around a smile. She looks even friendlier now she knows we're in hiding. Apparently, we're her kind of people.

On the walls are several posters featuring bands and their tour dates. My gaze catches on a familiar flaming logo and I grin. It's a Flaming Buttholes poster.

"You have good taste in music." I nod at it.

"Oh yeah, I love Jess's band." Morgan slaps Jess on the back. "Hey, I'd love to hang out with you guys, but I'm heading away for a few days. Got a gig in Philly, then another one upstate. My roommates went to pick up the truck, and when they get back, we're outta here."

"Do you mind if we stay while you're gone?" asks Jess. "We don't have anywhere else to go."

Morgan waves one hand. "Of course, babe. That's what I meant. You can look after the house for us. Not sure how long we'll be gone, but stay as long as you want. Best not to answer the door though, in case it's our landlord. The guy's a dick." Her gaze goes to my shoulder and her eyes light up. "Hey, is that your rat? Can I hold him?"

"Sure. His name's Ratticus."

She lifts one hand and Ratticus sniffs it suspiciously. "*Oh sure*," he says in my head. "*Just hand me to anyone. Don't bother checking with me first.*"

"You're such a boss," coos Morgan as he steps reluctantly into her palm. "You like belly rubs, Ratticus? Want me to rub your little furry belly?"

Ratticus immediately flips over, spreading his feet in the air.

Morgan laughs and strokes his belly. "You like that, don't you, boss?"

Xander and I exchange a look. Here's the answer to one of our problems.

"Hey, you think you could look after Ratticus when you get back?" I ask. "I mean, if we can't take him with us."

"That'd be dope." Morgan's bright eyes lift to mine. "But if we rock the gigs, they might book us an extra night or two. We might not be back here 'til next week."

I shrug. "Oh well. If it works out, then great. Otherwise, we'll take him with us."

Morgan bends her face to the rat nestled in her hand. "Hey little boss, you want to live with me when I get back? You can have all the belly rubs you want."

Ratticus turns his head to look at me. "*Finally,*" he says in my head. "*Somebody with the decency to ask my opinion and the knowledge to satisfy my needs. Was that really so difficult?*"

"I think he likes you better than he likes us." I tell Morgan.

"*What gave it away?*" Ratticus leans his head back on her fingers and closes his eyes. "*Oh yeah, that's the spot. Right there. That's it.*"

We hear the roar of a badly-tuned engine outside, before it coughs to a stop. "That sounds like the truck." Morgan gives Ratticus back to me, and flicks off the weird moaning music. "I've gotta split, babe. It's a long drive and we're already running late."

"Do you mind not telling the rest of the band that we're here?" asks Jess. "We're kind of on the run. Want to keep our location on the down low."

"You're in some serious shit, huh?" Morgan seems impressed, and I make a mental note to ask Jess where she met her. Maybe they were cell mates during Jess's brief stint in jail.

Jess nods. "Yeah, we're in pretty deep."

"Do the rest of the Buttholes know?"

"No." Jess drops her gaze. "Don't tell them, okay? They'd only worry."

"Mikey came to the gig we played last weekend. He said you'd been sick?"

"I'm better now."

Morgan winks. "Mikey'd help you with anything you asked him to."

I know where she's going with this. Mikey has been in love with Jess for as long as I've known him. Jess pretends she doesn't notice, and Mikey pretends he doesn't care. Morgan may as well save her breath, because Jess has resisted every attempt to push them together, even though I can tell she likes him back. The reason they're not already a couple is one of life's greatest mysteries.

"Sure he would." Jess sounds a little too casual. "So would everyone in the band, and I'd do anything for them as well."

A horn honks outside, and Morgan goes over to the window. "My roomies are coming in. You can hide in my room if you don't want them to see you." She leads the way down the hall, and we traipse after her into a messy bedroom. A black bedspread covers the king-sized bed, and the clothes strewn on the floor are all black. Her side lamps are skulls, and she has old-fashioned pictures of Bella Lugosi and Elvira on the walls. Red velvet curtains are half-pulled over the windows, blocking out most of the sunlight.

"It'll take us a while to pack everything into the van," she says. "Wait here until you hear us take off. The key's hidden under the front door mat. Leave it there if you go before I get back. Oh, and you'll need to sleep in here too. The roomies won't want strangers dirtying up their sheets."

"Won't your roommates be home tonight?" I ask before Morgan can shut the door.

"I room with my bass player and drummer. We'll all get back from the gig at the same time." She shuts the door, and we hear her shouting out down the hall, "Yeah, I'm coming. Just give me a sec, okay?"

Ratticus sighs. *"I'm going to miss her,"* he says. *"I haven't met anyone that smart in a long time."*

Looking around, I notice the skull lumps are glowing softly in the dim light. I raise my eyebrows at Xander, who shrugs.

Jess sits on the end of the bed, and the rest of us join her. Ratticus scratches my neck, taking longer than normal to settle into a comfortable position. Probably on purpose, because I'm ignoring him instead of rubbing his belly.

We can hear Morgan's roommates talking and laughing in the living room as they carry their equipment out to the truck, so we stay silent, waiting until they leave. Xander is next to me, close enough that I can breathe in his fresh, oaky scent, and feel his warmth. He grabs my hand in his, and I give his fingers a squeeze.

Rebecca looks around curiously, like we're in the strangest room she's ever seen. I guess she doesn't know much about goth metal, and Megan is practically the poster child. She has a pentacle-shaped mirror, and a silver-handled knife lying on the dresser. There's a studded neck choker next to it, black lipstick, and a bottle of black nail polish.

All the things a goth girl might need.

I try to imagine what the rest of the band looks like. Maybe we're being over cautious staying hidden like this, but I can't help but think of how quickly Dallas found us at the cabin and how he blew it up after we left. There was no reason to do that, except pure malicious spite.

Yeah, keeping our whereabouts a secret from as many people as possible is sensible. We're putting them in danger just by being in their house. If Dallas turns up, he won't think twice before killing them.

The quicker they leave the better.

Chapter Ten

As the truck roars away, I let out a relieved breath and stand up. "Anyone else hungry?" My stomach chooses that exact moment to rumble.

Jess stands up and rolls her shoulders. "Starving."

"*Me too,*" says Ratticus.

"Dinner time," agrees Jess.

"What are we going to do for food?" I ask.

"I saw a takeaway pizza place just down the road," suggests Xander.

"*I like pizza,*" says Ratticus.

"How do you know Morgan?" I ask Jess as we head into the living room. The band equipment is all gone, making the area look completely different. It's spacious now, and I can picture us relaxing here.

"Her band plays similar gigs to the Flaming Buttholes. At least what we used to play in the old days." She looks a bit awkward. In band-speak, she's just admitted that her band is doing rather well.

I smirk at Jess. "Before you got famous?"

She shoots me a mock glare. "We're not famous. We're

*in*famous." She's completely serious, and it makes me smirk even harder.

Xander throws an arm over my shoulder. "So, everyone keen on pizza?" he asks.

"Sounds perfect." I squeeze his waist. The thought of all that melted cheese is making my mouth water.

"Morgan's a good musician." Jess walks over to the stereo. "They need to practise more, and play a few more gigs. Then they'll be amazing."

Xander kisses the top of my head. "You can stay here. I'll go get the pizzas." He strides to the door and I wander to the window to make sure he drives away safely. Guess I'm half expecting Dallas to turn up, even though it's harder for him to track us now the council bond is broken.

Behind me, I hear Jess playing around with the stereo, then music starts pumping. It's a strange mix of punk, folk and metal, but I find myself tapping my fingers to the beat. Then the singer starts to sing about how her boyfriend left her, and I recognise Morgan's scratchy, ten-packs-a-day voice.

"She's the lead singer?" I ask.

"And the lead guitarist. Told you she was good."

Her voice *is* good. Soulful and haunting. I wander over to the stereo and flick through the CDs piled up beside it. Jess starts dancing next to me, then drags me into the middle of the room, bouncing around like she's in a mosh pit.

I stare at her for a second, ready to protest that we're in danger of being hunted down and killed, that the world is about to end, that it's hardly the time for dancing.

But of course, that's the perfect time to dance.

I let out a deep breath, feeling some of the tension ease out of my shoulders. Then I start moshing with her.

"Her band's really good!" I pant, jumping up and down

and shaking my head so my hair flies wildly around my face.

"I told you." Jess grins and jumps higher, banging her head so her blonde hair whips even more.

Rebecca is sitting on the couch, watching us warily. I'm used to being silly with Jess, used to getting up and dancing. But I have no idea if Rebecca has ever danced in her life. I doubt she's ever been to a concert. Not just that she's young, but living with a bunch of old, serious witches in the council chambers can't have been much fun. I've never seen her act like a normal kid, and that can't be healthy.

I dance over to her and grab her hands. Before she can do more than shake her head and give me a panicked look, I've pulled her to her feet.

"Come on, dance with us!" I drag her into the middle of the floor.

"I can't." She stands still, looking awkward.

Jess dances around behind her, not moshing anymore, but doing some kind of tribal-looking dance with lots of foot-stamping and butt shaking. "Come on Rebecca, relax. Nobody's watching."

Rebecca holds off for another second or two, then she moves her feet around She still looks stiff and tense.

"Let go," I tell her. "Don't worry about what you look like."

She keeps moving, and slowly loosens up, copying Jess and me as we compete to see who can do the stupidest dance. Soon we have her bouncing around between us, shaking her blonde hair over her face like she's been doing it her whole life.

The music stops and we stand there for a moment, all of us panting like we've just run a marathon.

"I know." I race over to the stereo, looking for the CD I spotted earlier. I stick it in and press play. My favourite song of all time comes pumping out through the speakers. Mikey's voice booms out. *I won't do what ya want. I won't be what ya make me. Hard as ya try, ya still can't break me.*

Jess laughs and rolls her eyes. "Don't you get enough of that at home?"

It's from the first Flaming Buttholes album and Mikey's voice sounds particularly good on this track. Jess pretends she's holding drumsticks, and plays along on a set of imaginary drums. Rebecca and I jump around, banging our heads.

Then the chorus starts, with Mikey screaming 'You're a butthole,' over and over, and I remember the last time I heard this song. The first time my magic surged, the day Sylvia was murdered.

Suddenly, I don't feel like dancing anymore.

Xander pushes the front door open, and the smell of pizza hits us. The Buttholes are still playing, and Xander makes a face in the directions of the stereo as he puts the pizza on the table.

"Don't tell me you like this too?" He shoots Rebecca a grimace, but it's obvious he's joking. "Am I the only one with any musical taste?"

"Hey!" Jess folds her arms. "Did you just insult my band?"

"Yeah. But I have pizza." He opens one of the boxes, and the delicious smell makes my stomach rumble even louder than the music.

"You're forgiven." She slides a grin in his direction and takes a seat at the table. I turn the stereo off and join the others. We're all hungry, and the pizza tastes every bit as good as it smells. I eat way too much, then groan happily about how full I am.

Ratticus eats so much, he falls asleep on his back on

one of the chairs, his paws sticking up like he's in a cartoon.

"While I was out, I got a few basic supplies." Xander nods at a carrier bag he left next to the door. "Toothbrushes for everyone."

"Think Morgan would mind if I looked for a towel so I can have a shower?" I ask Jess.

"I think she'd tell us to help ourselves." Jess stands up. "I'll put the leftovers in the fridge for the morning." She carries the half-empty boxes out to the kitchen and I hear cupboards open and close. Then she gasps and I feel a surge of power through our coven link. "Rebecca," she yells from the kitchen, her voice panicked. "Don't let me time travel!"

Rebecca's eyes turn white and I can feel her clamping down on Jess's magic, stifling it. But my own, dark magic is surging too. And though Jess is in another room, the coppery scent of blood is suddenly thick on my tongue.

So is my longing for Jess's amazing, potent, golden power.

Before I've thought about what I'm doing, I find myself on my feet, walking to the kitchen. Jess must have cut herself while she was cleaning up, and I can feel her magic pulsing from the wound. I can't access her power through our coven link, because the Veritas is pulling it away from me. But Jess's blood is flowing. Touching it will fill me with her power.

"I caught my finger on a sharp edge," calls Jess. "But I'm okay."

My body feels like it's on autopilot. The dark magic throbs inside my veins, begging to be free. It's so strong a need, I can barely think of anything else.

Jess looks around as I walk into the kitchen, and frowns.

"Are you okay, Saff? Your heart has sped up." She holds her hand over her chest. "It's weird, but I can feel it beating faster."

Then a heavy hand lands on my arm, stopping me from reaching out to grasp Jess's injured hand. I feel Xander's warmth behind me, but for a moment, I still try to pull away, to reach toward Jess's blood. It's calling to me, and I *need* to answer.

"I didn't understand how strong it was," lisps a soft voice behind Xander.

My need for Jess's power lessens.

I drag in a deep breath and turn my head to see the Veritas. Her eyes are still white, and she's using our coven link to dampen my dark magic's bloodlust, as well as keeping Rebecca from accidentally time travelling.

"What's the matter?" Jess glances from me, to Xander, to Rebecca. "Why does Saffy look weird?"

When neither Xander or Rebecca answer, I take another deep, shuddering breath, and step backward, away from Jess's still-bleeding hand. "It's my dark magic. Your blood is..." I wave my hand, searching for the right word. "Irresistible."

Jess's eyes widen, and she backs up, moving away from me until she's against the kitchen cupboards. "Oh." She grabs a dishcloth from the counter and pushes it down on her finger to staunch the bleeding. "Xander, can you take Saffy away? Maybe go look in the bathroom for a bandage?"

With the Veritas's help, I don't need Xander to pull me away from Jess. I step back under my own steam, heading into the living room and sinking onto the couch. With my head in my hands, I take several more breaths, fighting off the last of my bloodlust.

Is this what it will be like for me now? Every time I

sense blood, will I be helpless not to act like a starving vampire? And will it keep getting worse?

Xander sits next to me and puts his arm around me, pulling me close. I rest my head on his shoulder, taking comfort in his strength and warmth. "It'll be okay," he murmurs. "You'll see. We'll figure this out."

I appreciate he's trying to reassure me, but a sigh slips out. "Any ideas on how we can figure any of this out? Dallas is getting more powerful, which means the demon is getting stronger too. I can't control my craving for blood, Jess can't use her powers, and the Veritas is barely in her teens. I wish I didn't feel so hopeless right now, but I'm out of ideas."

His arm tightens around me and he doesn't say anything, just holds me.

Weirdly, it makes me feel a little better that he's not pretending to have any answers. My muscles slowly relax, and I close my eyes as a wave of tiredness creeps over me.

Outside, it's now dark. We've had a long, eventful day, and I feel like I've been stretched too thin and I'm on the edge of breaking down completely. "I think I might go to bed," I tell him. "We should rest while we can."

Before Xander can answer, another voice comes from the door. "Good idea. I'm tired, too." Rebecca comes in, her eyes back to normal. Behind her is Jess, her finger now bandaged.

"You okay, Saff?" asks Jess.

I nod. "Sorry. Didn't mean to…" I motion to her bandaged hand.

"It's okay. I know you can't help it." She shoves her thumbs in her pockets. "You and Xander should take the bed. Rebecca and I will take the couches in here."

Xander shakes his head. "I'll take the couch, and—"

"That'd be stupid," interrupts Jess. "I get that you want

to be chivalrous, like we're living in the eighteen hundreds or something, but Rebecca and I are both small enough to fit comfortably on the couches. You'd be hanging off the edge."

"She's right," I tell Xander, because he still looks like he wants to argue. "Come on." I get to my feet and offer him my hand.

After a moment's hesitation, he takes it and we bid the others goodnight.

After showering, we snuggle together in Morgan's bed. But as many times as I've fantasised about getting to spend another night with Xander, I'm so exhausted and heart-sick, I can't bring myself to do more than curl up with his arm around me.

He seems to know exactly how I feel, because he just kisses me gently, holding me close.

"I don't know what I'd do without you," I tell him quietly. In the darkness, it feels like a confession.

"I'm not going anywhere." His low voice rumbles in my ear.

"You sure?" It makes me feel vulnerable to ask, but I can't help myself. "Even if the dark magic gets worse?"

"I'm here, Saff. Always. No matter what."

I let out a long breath. "I love you," I whisper. Then I close my eyes and let the heaviness of sleep take me away.

Chapter Eleven

Someone is screaming.

Great terrible gut-wrenching screams dig into my brain, cutting through the haze of sleep.

I force my eyes open.

I'm standing up, not lying down. I must have leapt out of bed before I was fully awake.

The room is dark, only illuminated by moonlight coming in through the window. I'm standing over the couch in the living room. Below me is Jess, her mouth open in a terrified scream. Her eyes are wide with fear, and she's staring at me. *Screaming* at me.

On the other couch, the Veritas sits up. Her expression is almost as shocked as Jess's, and she stares at me too, fear in her eyes. As though she's afraid of me.

Frowning with confusion, I try to figure out what's happening. Why is Jess screaming? What's she so terrified of?

And then I see the silver-handled knife, the one from Morgan's dresser. It's in my hand, and I'm holding it high, as if I'm about to swing it down.

Into Jess's beating heart.

My dark magic is churning inside me. It wants to feast on Jess's intoxicating golden power. I can see it so clearly in my head, how I would plunge the knife into her heart, how my power would surge, how taking Jess's life would make me stronger than I've ever been in my life.

The longing for power aches inside me, and I want to throw up.

I drop my hand, letting go of the knife, and hear it clatter onto the floor. "I'm sorry, Jess. I didn't... It's not..."

The living room light flicks on, and I blink in the sudden brightness.

"What's going on?" Xander's voice comes from behind me. "Jess? What's wrong?" He strides in and drops to his knees beside the couch she's lying on. "Did you have a bad dream?"

"It was Saffy." Jess scrambles off the couch, backing away from me.

"Saffy?" Xander gets up and puts his hand on my arm. "What happened? What were you doing?" The worry in his voice makes me feel even worse.

Instead of answering, I look at Rebecca who's still sitting on the other couch. "Can you feel it inside me?" I ask. "The blood lust?"

She nods. "It's so strong, I can barely feel anything else."

"I don't know what happened." I look down at the knife on the floor, squeezing my hands into fists as my fingers start to tremble. "I went to sleep, then I woke up standing over Jess."

"You don't remember getting out of bed?" asks Xander.

I shake my head, trying to get the visions of blood out

of my mind. "I was asleep. I had no idea the dark magic could take over like that."

Jess is still keeping her distance. "Your eyes were completely black," she says. "What if I hadn't woken up? Would I be dead right now?"

The question hits me hard. I can't be trusted. I've been terrified of the dark magic turning me into someone evil like the Unseen, but I thought it would be later. I thought I had more time. But it's happening already and the reality of it is worse than I imagined.

"I'm sorry," I whisper. I don't know what else to say. I feel like my heart is breaking.

Xander puts his arm around me. "Now that we know it can influence you, we'll take precautions." His tone is gentle. "You're stronger than this thing. I know you are."

"I don't know if I am," I whisper, my voice raw. "What if it gets worse? What if I stop being able to control it when I'm awake? "

The Veritas clears her throat into the tense silence. "I wasn't going to tell you about the vision I had in the car. But now I need to."

I shiver, suddenly cold. Xander hugs me tighter, but there's nothing he can do to warm me. This cold is coming from inside, from my dread of what she's about to say.

"Tell us," demands Jess.

The Veritas shifts awkwardly, as if she's trying to find a comfortable spot, except there isn't one. "The vision was of you, Saffy."

I swallow hard, trying to imagine what she could have seen. "Was I dead?"

She shakes her head. "You were with the demon." she says in a rush. "Helping it create chaos and murder innocent people."

Another chill runs through me. "No, it's not true. There's no way I'd help the demon."

"It can't possibly be true." Xander sounds angry.

Rebecca looks sad. "My visions aren't wrong. That's what's going to happen."

"Can we stop it?" Jess asks.

I pull away from Xander, too restless to stand still. "If we can find a way to contain the demon, we can keep the vision from happening, can't we?"

Rebecca gives a small shrug. "Maybe."

"Then that's what we have to do." I stalk to the window, pushing aside the curtains to stare sightlessly outside. I can't bear to look at any of them. How could I lose myself so totally that I would join the demon in killing people? It doesn't seem possible.

But just a few moments ago, I was holding a knife over Jess's heart. So it's definitely possible.

"You found a way to get the demon out of me, Saff." Xander takes a step toward me. "Everyone said that was impossible, but you did it. You'll beat this too."

"This isn't just people saying it's impossible," says Jess. "This is literally a vision of the actual future we're dealing with."

"How set in stone are your visions?" demands Xander.

The Veritas shakes her head. "I've never had them like this before. Until now, they've been few and far between. But every time I'm close to Saffy, I seem to get them."

"So now we have a coven connection, they're likely to come thick and fast?" The thought's disturbing. I've experienced a couple of the Veritas's visions, and they weren't a barrel of chuckles.

"Are you sure that Saffy was helping the demon?" Xander's using his detective voice. "Describe your vision to us in as much detail as possible. Maybe it'll help us discover how to fight it."

"I can do better than describe it." Rebecca nods at him. "Take Saffy's hands."

He does what she asks, gripping both of my hands. I know what's going to come next, and I want to protest. I don't want to see what she did.

But I have to.

I need to know for sure.

Rebecca closes her eyes, and I can feel her magic reaching out to me through our coven link. She's sending the vision to me and Jess, and with Xander holding my hands, I can only assume he'll experience it too.

For a moment, white fills my vision.

Then the white turns into darkness. It's night time. But the sky is both red and black with flames and smoke.

The demon is in front of a burning building. It stinks like wet dog and rotting meat, its stench drifting over the smell of burning. Behind it, people are burning to death, their screams shrill over the roar of the fire.

I'm standing next to the demon. My hands are stretched out and on the ground in front of me is the crumpled, bloody body of a woman. She must be a witch, because I'm absorbing her power, dragging strands of magic out of her like I'm unravelling the wool from an unwanted piece of knitting.

My skin is grey, and my eyes are so black they look like sinkholes.

The strangest thing is that this terrible version of me in the vision is wearing jeans and my favourite Flaming Butt-holes t-shirt.

It makes it seem real.

It makes it seem like it's actually happening.

Then, just like that, the vision vanishes, and I'm back in Morgan's living room with the others.

I put my hand to my mouth to stop the bile that's burning up through my throat. The demon's stench is still in my nose, and the screams of the dying echo in my head.

I used to think I was a good person.

Not anymore.

The demon's power tempted me before, and now I know I'll eventually give in to it, and let myself become pure evil.

"Shit," breathes Xander.

I turn my face away from him so I can't see his expression. He'll never look at me the same way again. Neither will Jess. I won't blame them if they want nothing to do with me anymore. Hell, *I* don't want anything to do with me.

"We can't let that happen." Xander sounds angry. "Tell us how to stop it."

"There has to be a way," agrees Jess.

I drag my gaze off the floor to meet Rebecca's eyes. "If it looks like that's going to happen, you need to kill me before it does." My voice comes out flat but determined. "Promise me you will."

"No!" protests Xander, but Rebecca nods.

"I promise." Her expression is serious, and I can't help but believe her. She's young, and is small enough to look fragile, but she's also a powerful Veritas, devoted to the truth and capable of powerful magic.

I'm pretty sure she could kill me if she put her mind to it. More importantly, I trust her to keep her word.

"Thank you," I tell her.

Chapter Twelve

No one talks as we sit at the table, eating cold pizza for breakfast. Even Ratticus is mostly quiet for a change, sitting on one of the chairs with us, a slice of pizza clutched in his front paws. Except for a few loud sighs, and making it clear that he can't wait for Morgan—*the smart one*—to return, he's so far refrained from commenting about the night's events.

We're all involved in our own thoughts, and when Jess speaks, it makes me jump.

"Where did Jeqabeel come from?" she asks.

"My mother had its thigh bone. Its essence was trapped in the bone."

Jess frowns. "How did she get it?"

"Your mother's ancestors were part of the coven that trapped Jeqabeel." The Veritas's voice is flat. She hasn't looked me in the eyes since she promised to kill me.

"Let's go over everything we know about it," says Xander. "Maybe it'll trigger an idea for getting rid of the demon without Saffy becoming his sidekick."

I nod. "My mother was proud of the artefact. It came down through my family."

"Then let's start there."

Sliding back in my seat, I close my eyes to picture my mother sitting at her desk in her office. She used to research and record the history of some of the hundreds of magical artefacts she had in her safe, and she'd sometimes tell me about them while she worked.

"This one, Saffy. This one is amazing," she'd say, her smile wide, blue eyes dancing, holding up an ugly dog statue with a fat belly and a long snout. "It's a fertility dog used by a sub-tribe of the Mayans. They believed it would help the women of the tribe become pregnant. Can you feel the magic?"

I used to roll my eyes, and pretend I was embarrassed, but really, I used to love how enthusiastic she'd get.

In fact, now that I think about it, I do remember her holding up a bone that was encased in plastic. I remember her warning me never to touch it.

"She knew it was dangerous," I say.

"Your mother sounds like a genius," mutters Ratticus. *"Now I know where you inherited your astonishing brain power."* He swallows the last of his pizza and lies down with a satisfied groan.

"What else?" asks Xander.

I wrack my brains, trying to think what else she said that day. "She said it was a family heirloom, that it had been handed down through the female line. It was our responsibility to keep it safe." I realise now that I never took that seriously, didn't understand how dangerous the bone actually was.

"Anything else?" asks Xander. When I shake my head, he looks at the Veritas. "What do you know about Jeqabeel?"

"Almost nothing," she says. "Only what I've seen in my visions, and I've already shared those with you."

"And you?" he asks Jess.

"I'd never even heard of Jeqabeel before the Unseen tied me up in his basement." Jess tugs her phone out of her pocket. "I only have a tiny bit of charge left, but has anyone Googled it yet?" Without waiting for an answer, she starts looking it up.

"What did Mireya say about Jeqabeel?" I ask Xander. "Do you remember?"

He nods slowly. "She said the last time it was loose, it killed a lot of people. In the eighteen hundreds, wasn't it?"

"All I can remember is the picture she showed us. Wasn't the Library of Congress in it? The demon had destroyed it."

Jess looks up from her phone. "Hey, look at this." She turns it around so we can see the video that's playing.

It's Dallas. He's dressed in a dark suit, on a stage in front of a black curtain. The contrast makes his white hair and skin look even more startling than usual. He's wearing dark glasses, presumably to hide the glow of his eyes, and he's standing next to Xander's mother, Mayor Trent. There's a podium in front of her, and she's speaking into a microphone, making some sort of announcement.

"What the hell?" Xander mutters.

Jess turns up the volume. Mayor Trent looks flustered and a little dishevelled, with her normally perfect hairstyle a little messy and her cheeks flushed. "To counteract this spate of murders, we're putting a city-wide curfew in place." She holds up her hand as reporters shout out to her. "We don't know what kind of criminal organisation might be behind them. But we're taking strict measures to ensure the public's safety."

She glances sideways at Dallas as though checking for

his approval, then continues. "The sad and untimely death of Robert Arbour left us all shaken. But it is with great pleasure that I'm able to announce his replacement. A new Deputy Mayor who will live up to Robert's high standards. Dallas Oswolde has my complete support in his new position, and will be focusing primarily on security until this situation is resolved. I've authorized him to implement bold new emergency policies to combat the violence. And now he'll tell you about those policies."

She steps back, smiling and clapping as Dallas takes her place at the microphone. Following her lead, the assembled audience claps too.

"Thank you, Mayor Trent," says Dallas. "As you know, we're facing uncertain times. In recent days, our crime rate has skyrocketed, with fresh atrocities being committed at a rate we've never seen. Last night alone, more than a hundred people were found murdered. Their bodies were mutilated, their blood drained. We believe it's the work of a highly organised gang or cult, and a specialized task force is following up strong leads. However, until the perpetrators of these heinous crimes are in custody, we need to place restrictions on our community. To keep all citizens safe, we're imposing a city-wide curfew. Effective immediately."

Dallas pauses as a murmur runs through the assembled crowd. A few reporters start shouting questions, but he holds his hands up for silence. When the mutters die away, he keeps talking. "All citizens must be at home by 10pm every evening. No one may leave their homes before 7am in the morning. All bars, restaurants, and clubs will have a mandatory 9.30pm closing time, and night shift workers will need to contact their employers for new working hours. I've set up a phone line for questions and we'll be working closely with businesses to help them comply with the restrictions."

The crowd is getting louder. Murmurs are turning to shouts.

Again, Dallas holds up his hands for silence, and once more the crowd grudgingly and slowly quietens.

"It's vital that everyone obeys this curfew, for their own safety and for the safety of the police officers who will be patrolling our streets. Strict penalties will be enforced."

"But why do we need a curfew?" one eager reporter shouts. "Is there something you're not telling us?"

"We've never experienced violence on the scale of the murders that we've seen in the past few days. If we don't take drastic action, the number of deaths won't be in the hundreds. It'll be in the *thousands*."

Xander makes a shocked sound in the back of his throat. He looks as horrified as I feel.

Jess's phone flashes up a battery warning, and she swipes the message away. "It's just about out of juice, and I don't have a charger."

"Dallas is taking over the city," I say.

"Worse than that," says Xander. "He's the one doing the killing and he's using it as an excuse to control everyone."

I swallow bile at Dallas's utter fiendishness. "He's a smart guy. Whatever we decide to do, we have to remember that."

"He's draining blood from his victims," says Rebecca. "Jeqabeel is using it to gather power."

I nod, remembering Uncle Ray doing the same thing in the nightclub we visited. He created a river of blood to give Jequabeel the strength to create its own physical body.

"Listen," says Jess, turning the screen to face us. "He's talking again."

"…a bed for every citizen," Dallas is saying. "Volunteers will collect the homeless and bring them into one of our newly created shelters. Nobody will be left unprotected on the streets."

"I think he's rounding everyone up," lisps Rebecca. "So he can take their blood more easily."

"He must be doing something to my mother, or she wouldn't let him go ahead with this." Xander glances at me. "I mean, I know she's not exactly up for Mother of the Year, but she's usually pretty savvy. This is madness."

"He must be controlling her," I agree.

"We can't let him round up and kill all the homeless people." Jess is clutching her phone so hard her fingers are going white.

"How do we stop him?" I ask. "He's way more powerful than we are."

The screen of Jess's phone goes black. "It's dead." She makes a sound of frustration in the back of her throat and stands up. "There's only one way to stop him. I"ll use my time travel powers to kill—"

"No." The Veritas shakes her head. "We can't risk you using your power when we know so little about it. What if you change the timeline and accidentally destroy the entire country?"

Jess lifts her chin, her expression set. "I have to do something. What if I can go back in time and lock Dallas in a basement? Surely that won't disrupt the timeline."

"But we know nothing about your power," insists Rebecca. "We have no idea if it would be dangerous to do that."

"She's right. You've only just discovered your power, and until we can find out more about it, you shouldn't use it." I drag in a deep breath. "It should be me. I'll use my dark magic to face Dallas. I beat the Unseen, I can beat him too."

Xander shakes his head. "No way. Your dark magic is already taking you over. Using it will only make that happen faster."

I put my hand on his arm. "That's actually a good reason why I should do it." I keep my voice gentle, willing him to understand. "I'm going down the dark path already. If Dallas manages to kill me…"

"You're not going to die for the rest of us." Xander folds him arms. "That's final."

"What if it's the only way?" I ask.

He shakes his head, his mouth set. "You didn't give up on me, and I'm not giving up on you."

His ice blue eyes gaze into mine, and instead of being comforting, I'm afraid he can see the darkness inside me. I'm turning into a monster, and I don't want him to see me like this.

"What about Rebecca's vision?" asks Jess. "If Dallas captures you, he could use your dark magic to bring you onto his side. You could make her vision come true."

"The plan is obvious," lisps Rebecca.

We all turn to her. For a teenager with a lisp, she can be surprisingly authoritative. Old beyond her years.

"I'll face Dallas, and turn him to stone," she says. "That should trap the demon inside him."

"You think you're strong enough to do that?" I ask. It's a decent idea, and for the first time I feel a surge of hope. I remember all too well how awful it was to be turned into a statue. The the idea of Dallas suffering the same fate is appealing.

"If I draw on your magic." Rebecca looks between me and Jess. "I can use the coven link to direct all of our power into the spell. But it'll be easier to use your power if all three of us face him together."

"But Jess has no protection," I point out. "She can't fight with her magic."

Jess shoots me a frown. "Don't worry about me. I can handle myself."

"We'd need to get Dallas alone." Xander sounds as hopeful as I feel. "So we don't have to fight off other witches at the same time."

"How do we find him?" I ask.

"He's been sleeping at the Council Chambers," says Rebecca.

"So we break into the chambers in the middle of the night while everyone's asleep." Xander sounds thoughtful. "You'll need to tell us everything you know. How many other witches sleep there, whether guards are posted, any other defences."

"You can't come in with us." Rebecca faces him, her tone firm. "The three of us will face Dallas."

"No way."

"She's right," I tell him. "As great as you are in any other situation, you're helpless against magic. You won't be able to help us."

He shakes his head, his expression stubborn. "You're not going in without me."

"There'll be guards on the doors," says Rebecca. "We'll need you to create a distraction and draw them away so we can sneak inside."

"We'll have to get the car to somewhere near the Council Chambers before the curfew, and then hide in it until it's dark," says Jess.

"We're going to do this tonight?" I ask, standing up. Now that we've got a plan, I feel better. At least we're doing something, even if it might get us all killed.

"*You're forgetting something important*," says Ratticus, still lolling on the chair. "*The smart one might be away for several days. You have to stay here until she gets back, or I might run out of food.*"

I look over at his bulging belly. "You have two choices, Ratticus. Either take your chances here, waiting for Morgan to come back. Or you can come with us."

Chapter Thirteen

"*This sucks*," grumbles Ratticus.

I have to agree. My legs are aching, and though night has fallen, the car is stuffy and I'm too hot. All I want to do is stretch.

We're parked about a ten minute walk from the Blood Council Chambers. Xander stole—or rather, borrowed—a car with tinted windows and we've parked in a dark, secluded spot on one of the narrow, quiet roads running through Druid Hill Park. We're surrounded by nothing but trees. Even so, we're keeping as low as we can, just in case. Maybe we're being paranoid, but with the Council Chambers so close, none of us want to take any chances. Besides, the official curfew is in place and if anyone happens to spot us, we'll be in serious trouble.

"How much longer?" I ask.

"It's only been five minutes since the last time you asked." Jess sounds testy. She's crouched in the footwell of the front passenger seat, and doesn't look any more comfortable than I am. We parked here before the curfew started, and since then it's grown properly dark. It feels like we've been here for at least three hours. Maybe longer.

I let out an impatient huff of breath. Then a heel digs into my side.

"Ow!"

"Sorry," says Xander. "I've got pins and needles." His huge body is crammed in next to mine. He has more room than I do, but then again, he's a man mountain. Far too big and tall to be squashed into the back seat with me.

"Don't we all," I mutter, mostly to take my mind off his body. Now's definitely not the time to be recalling just how wide his chest is, or how good it feels to run my hands over it, only it's hard not to dwell on those things when he's pressed so close.

"It's too hot in here." Ratticus clambers onto my arm, his claws scratching my skin. *"And demon dude almost rolled on me."*

"What time is it?" asks Rebecca. As the smallest of us, we assigned her the driver's seat, so she's wedged awkwardly under the steering wheel.

"Time to go," says Xander. "I'd rather face the demon than spend any more time in this car."

"I'd rather you faced the demon too," agrees Ratticus. *"I should have taken my chances waiting for the smart one."*

Xander opens the door, groaning with relief as he climbs out.

I drag myself out behind him, barely able to feel my legs. "Stay here," I murmur to Ratticus. "We'll be back soon."

"Like I was tempted to come with you."

Keeping low, I shut the door and crouch behind the car.

"I still object to this plan," Xander murmurs into my

ear. "I hate the thought of you going in without me." He catches my hand and squeezes it. "Be careful, okay?"

I steal a quick kiss. "You too."

"Let's go." He heads off at a low jog, leading us along the edge of the forest. I stick close behind him with Jess and Rebecca at my heels. I'm clutching the silver-handled knife from Morgan's dresser. The same one I almost used on Jess.

As we approach the council chambers, I can't help but think how crazy this is. We're sneaking into the last place we should want to go, to find the demon that wants to suck out our power to help him destroy the world. Hopefully, it's the last thing Dallas will expect.

We circle around to the back of the mansion and crouch in the tree line, peering through the dark night to the back door.

"Two guards," whispers Xander. "I'm up." He touches my hand softly, and I wish it weren't so dark so he could see my face more clearly, and make out the soulful look I'm giving him. This is dangerous for all of us, and I'm more afraid for him than I am for myself.

Then he turns to the Veritas. "Ready," he whispers.

She takes his hands and I see her magic curl into him, white strands twisting around his body. I can feel it too, and sense what she's doing. She's not actually changing him, just distorting the way the guards will see him. Using her power to change their perception of him.

"The guards will see multiple versions of you, and the copies will be in lines, in front of you and to the sides," whispers the Veritas. "The fake Xanders will do whatever you do, but in a slightly different direction, so you don't all look exactly the same. Keep moving, and you won't get hit."

Before I can tell him again to be careful, Xander slips

away, running quickly across the small expanse of lawn at the back of the house. There's a strange shimmer behind him, and threads of the spell wave like tentacles over his body. The idea is that the guards will focus on what will look like a group of approaching men, and we'll be able to use the distraction to get inside.

Sure enough, there's a shout, then a flash as a fireball cuts through the night, whizzing past Xander. The other guard shoots glittering ice shards like shining bullets, and my heart leaps into my throat. Those things are lethal. But the witches are targeting something only they can see, at the wrong angle to hit the real Xander.

Xander ducks and dodges, and presumably his copies do the same. The guards are looking overwhelmed, as if they're seeing too many Xanders to count. He cuts toward the side of the building, as though he's heading to the mansion's front doors, and the guards give chase.

My heart is beating too fast, and every time a missile flies too close to him, I have to fight the urge to jump up and yell at him to watch out. But it's working. The two witches are following him away from the building's back door, still firing fire and ice as they try desperately to bring down the elusive runners in front of them.

As Xander disappears around the side of the building with the witches at his heels, I spring to my feet.

"Come on." I break from the cover of the trees, and sprint to the back door with Jess and the Veritas behind me. The door is locked, but all I need is a drop of blood to unlock it with my earth magic.

When we slip inside, the long hallway looks exactly the same as I remember from when Rebecca released me from the statue spell. Only difference is that this time we're heading into danger, instead of escaping from it.

"Are you sure you know where Dallas will be?" I

whisper to Rebecca. I'm holding my knife out in front of me, because carrying it makes me feel a little better about creeping down long, dark hallways that could be filled with witches who want to kill us. I'm gripping its handle so hard I think its decorative ridges might be permanently tattooed into my palm, but I can't seem to talk my fingers into loosening their grip.

"I've lived here most of my life," Rebecca whispers back. "I know where I'm going."

My eyes have adjusted to the gloom, and there's some light coming in the high windows from the almost-full moon. Beside me, Jess is also carrying a knife in front of her, ready to stab anyone we meet. Rebecca's knife is no doubt tucked away in a handy pocket, because she knows she won't need to cut anyone but herself. I shoot Jess a half smile. Our mundane upbringing is showing.

Rebecca leads us down the hallway, round corners, and through another couple of doors. We head up a dark, narrow staircase that might have once been a servants' entrance. About half way up, I manage to trip over my own feet and my shoe thumps the stair riser.

"Shhh," hisses Rebecca. "We're close."

I shift the knife into my other hand, stretching my stiff fingers. With the coven link controlling my dark magic, I'm pretty much helpless. But if I drove my blade into Rebecca's back, her blood would ignite my power and…

Wait. What am I thinking?

The dark magic is affecting my thoughts. Will I eventually lose control altogether? And if that happens, will I be too far gone to let Rebecca kill me? It creeps me out to imagine myself turning into a creature like the Unseen.

Rebecca stops in front of a large vaulted wooden door. "This is it," she whispers.

The three of us exchange a look, all drawing in a deep

breath, readying ourselves for what might be on the other side.

Then I push open the door.

It's a bedroom. A large window lets in enough light to make out a lump in the king-sized bed. Judging by the gentle snores reaching my ears, whoever it is must be fast asleep.

My heart leaps in my chest. Could it be Dallas? Have we found him?

It seems strange the demon would allow Dallas to sleep, but at the end of the day, he's still human. I guess Jeqabeel doesn't want its host to go completely crazy. At least, not until the demon has its own physical body and doesn't need Dallas anymore.

There's nobody else in the room. We couldn't have asked for a better chance for Rebecca to perform her spell, but it seems too good to be true. Why weren't there guards on the door? Is the demon that confident of its power?

Rebecca pushes past me, stepping softly into the room. She and Jess are both pale, but they look determined. Swallowing my doubts, I ease in behind them and gently close the door.

The three of us tiptoe to the bed. Rebecca pulls her knife out of her pocket and her magic tugs on mine. She gathers my power, using the coven link to pull it to her.

The door opens behind us.

I whirl around as the overhead light flicks on. Every muscle in my body goes tight. The creature standing in the doorway has the body of a man, clothed in dark, rumpled clothes, but the head of a jackal. Though its head is black and hairy, its hands are pale and human. They're Dallas's hands.

Beside me, Jess sucks in a gasp. Rebecca takes several steps backward, until the bed blocks her from going any further. I don't blame her. The demon is no less terrifying now than when I last saw it like this, when it had taken control of Uncle Ray's body.

"Welcome." Its voice is human with a hint of a rough, animal-like growl. "I was hoping you'd come." Then its stench hits me, making me gag and cover my nose.

"Dad," whispers Jess, her tone horrified.

I follow her gaze behind us, to the figure in the bed. Magnus is dragging himself out from under the covers. His movements are slow, and his eyes are glazed and distant. He hasn't responded to the sound of Jess's voice, and I'm pretty sure he's not in control of his mind.

"You're back where you belong," growls the demon. "The three of you will rejoin the Blood Council." Its canine eyes focus on me. "You will cause me no more trouble. Now you'll obey my will."

I lift my chin, not wanting to show my fear. "Think I'll pass. I've never been much of a joiner."

The creature steps closer, its stench growing even stronger. Its eyes are so black that looking into them is like staring into pits that reach all the way to hell. It lifts its arms, and I can only brace myself for whatever it's about to do.

Then I feel my magic being yanked out of me. Rebecca is drawing hard on my power through the coven link. Her hands are red with blood, and her eyes have turned pure white. She's captured the demon's black gaze.

Just as we planned, she's using her Veritas magic to bring the creature under her control and turn Dallas to stone.

Chapter Fourteen

White strands of glowing magic extend from the Veritas, reaching toward the demon.

As soon as I realize what she's doing, I push all my magic through the coven bond to her, holding nothing back. I can feel Jess doing the same.

Could this really work? Can Rebecca turn Dallas into a living statue, trapping the demon in his body?

Rebecca's magic is so bright, it hurts my eyes. She's immensely powerful, especially with Jess's and my magic added to hers. It doesn't seem possible that one small girl could contain that much power. The air hums with energy and all my hair stands on end. It feels like the entire room could explode.

This has to work. Not even a demon could resist so much magic.

But the jackal's eyes aren't black anymore. They've turned a vivid blood-red, as if the magma from the centre of the earth has flared up through the darkness. Dallas's pale hands clench, then a wave of dark energy pulses out from the demon.

The shockwave slams into me. All three of us fly backward, and I smack hard against the rough stone wall, my knife flying out of my hand. My shoulder scrapes against the stone, sloughing off my skin. Blood wells and my magic surges.

My magic's free.

Rebecca used up most of it on her spell, but what's left rises inside me, unconfined by the coven link. Rebecca's lying limp on the floor, a little blood seeping from her nose. She's been knocked out, and her control over me has released.

Jess is lying motionless next to her, and I'm not sure whether she's conscious either. If I could reach either one and take their blood, I could use my dark magic.

First, I need to distract the demon so I can reach them. My own blood will only feed my regular magic, which isn't nearly as strong as the dark magic.

Holding my animal magic in with a rune, I pour my earth magic into the heavy stone blocks that make up most of the building. The stone breaks, huge blocks crashing down, aimed squarely at Dallas.

But they don't hit him.

The demon's dark magic rises around him, black tentacles writhing. The stone vaporises, turned to dust.

Hands grab me from behind. *Magnus.*

"Let me go!" Even as I struggle, I can feel the demon's power pulsing toward me. Magnus has a grip like iron around my arms, holding me still.

The demon's magic is dark and strong. My dark magic rises in response, drawn to Jeqabeel's power. It's attracted to the demon, like a cat to catnip. It wants to rub itself against its magic and purr.

The demon's power reaches me and it feels every bit as

good as I'd hoped. For a moment, I'm exultant. Every cell in my body aches for my dark magic to merge with the demon's. I long for the power it showed me. To feel that incredible rush of energy pulse through my veins once more.

Bile rises in my throat as I realize I've stopped struggling. That I'm standing still, my palms open, welcoming Jequabeel's demonic magic. *Encouraging* it.

Then a stinging pain bursts through my brain, and a dark, oily heaviness settles over me.

It tightens around me until my entire body is stiff.

I can't move.

I can't talk, or blink, or even twitch a finger.

A wave of panic floods through me. A scream of horror rises up in my throat, unable to escape. I spent what felt like endless years as a statue, and now I'm frozen once more.

This can't be happening. I'd rather die than be a statue again.

I'm panting, my breaths coming so fast, it feels like I'm sprinting instead of standing still. But the fact I can breathe at all gives me something to cling to.

This isn't as bad as being a statue. I can't move my limbs, but at least I'm not locked off from the world, and I can see and hear.

"Bring all three down to the main chamber," Jeqabeel growls.

In response, more witches pour into the room. They must have been waiting outside. This whole thing was an ambush. Jeqabeel lured us in here, and the sea of witches who've appeared are proof that the demon made sure we couldn't escape.

We never stood a chance.

Witches lift me up and bundle me out the door. As we

pass Rebecca, I see more witches lifting her. She's still not moving, and there's blood on her face.

Jess is conscious now, and her eyes are wide. But she's frozen too. Whatever the demon did to me, it also did to her. As the witches who are carrying me jostle me down the hallway, I catch a glimpse of her behind us, being dragged along as roughly as I am.

They haul the three of us into the council's main chamber, and set me down on my feet inside one of the nine circles etched into the floor.

They've illuminated the room with fire torches around the walls, and moonlight is shining through the large skylight, far overhead. The flickering, eerie light makes it look even more ominous, but even if it were the middle of the day, this room brings back such bad memories, I'd still have the same sensation of icy fingers painfully squeezing my heart.

The witches place Jess carefully inside another of the nine circles, the one next to mine. She stands stiffly, her head locked into place, looking straight ahead so I can't see her face. She also has small cuts and grazes on her arms, wounds from being thrown around the room. She's so close that if I could move, I'd be able to reach out and take her blood to feed my dark magic. The thought makes me ache with longing and my muscles strain against the demon's invisible binding. My dark magic would be no match for Jeqabeel's power, but my thirst for blood isn't fully rational. And being around the demon makes the longing harder to suppress.

The witches lie Rebecca down in a third circle. She must have taken a hard blow to the head to be still unconscious, and her pale, fragile-looking limbs are also scraped and bruised. The three of us are in a sorry state, but it's the fact she's still knocked out that has me most worried.

The other members of the Blood Council take their places. Magnus steps into one circle, as do four other witches I don't recognize. They walk together like synchronized puppets, their eyes blank.

I'm pretty sure that's what will happen to us once the ceremony is complete. The demon will control us, body and mind. The thought makes me struggle against the demon's bonds again.

Jeqabeel is in the final circle, where the head of the council stands. The demon looks even more menacing in this room, with the flickering light playing over its ugly black jackal face. At least its eyes aren't glowing red anymore. But the black magic that seethes and writhes around it seem to swallow all traces of light. Dallas has been lost inside the power of the demon.

One of the attending witches moves toward me with a ceremonial knife and a goblet. I recognize her as someone my mother used to know, an older woman with long silver hair. But any faint hope she might help us dies when I see her eyes are as blank as all the others.

She slices my finger and collects my blood in the goblet. My magic surges as my blood flows, but it can't escape whatever spell the demon has wrapped tightly around me.

When she has enough of my blood, the silver-haired witch moves on to Jess, and then to Rebecca. Finally, the other council members contribute some of their blood to the mix. All except Jeqabeel.

I remember this ceremony from when Uncle Ray tried to unleash the demon. The council members all drank each other's blood to strengthen their link, then Ray fed their shared magic to Jeqabeel.

Uncle Ray needed the Blood Moon to give him enough power for Jeqabeel's transformation. But the demon is in Dallas's body now, and Dallas's magic is far stronger than Ray's was. The demon probably has good reason to think the ceremony will work under the light of a regular moon. It'll have the power of the entire council to draw on, including the Veritas, Jess, and me. Not to mention the rivers of mundane blood it's been drawing power from.

While the silver-haired witch collects the last of the blood she needs to fill the goblet, Dallas strips off his shirt. The jackal's hairy neck disappears into Dallas's bony white shoulders, the demon's black magic oozing over both like snakes pulled from shadows. The sight is both grotesque and horrifying.

Dallas lifts a knife in both hands and carves a large circle into his own chest. Blood wells from the wound, dribbling down his lily-white skin, but he shows no sign of pain. He keeps cutting, filling the circle with symbols that become indecipherable as blood fills the cuts. Without once looking down, he turns his initial circle into what is probably an intricate rune, but from here looks like a gory, bloody mess.

When he's done, he drops the knife, letting it clatter to the floor, and motions the silver-haired witch forward with the goblet. She holds it under his wounds. As Dallas's blood drips into the goblet, the demon's magic twists in with it, strands of oily blackness that make the blood hiss and boil.

The silver-haired witch passes the goblet to Magnus. My gut roils as he sips its contents. Tendrils of magic push out from his chest, extending like long fingers toward Dallas. At the same time, Magnus seems to age, his long beard becoming grayer and his face more lined, as though his life-force is being pulled out of him along with his power.

When Magnus's magic tendrils reach him, oily black smoke oozes from the rune carved into Dallas's chest.

The silver-haired witch passes the goblet to the next council member to sip from, and then the next. More tendrils of magic extend toward Dallas. The demon is feeding on their magic, sucking it into itself to fuel its transformation.

The council members age in front of my eyes. Their thin bodies become more frail, and their lined faces sag.

The smoke forms a dark mass behind Dallas. It's solidifying quickly. The demon's transformation is happening faster than when Uncle Ray performed the same ceremony. Only this time, I'm not as repulsed by Jeqabeel's true form taking shape behind Dallas. Deep inside me, my dark magic is surging, attracted to the demon's magic, even as I try to deny it.

Dallas's face changes, his jackal snout and hair disappearing. His white hair is back, and his own, human face. Only he's aged too. His eyes are sunken into his skull and he looks like a walking skeleton.

"Give the blood to her." Dallas speaks with the demon's growl still, though his voice has become even more guttural, and the words are hard to make out.

He points one pale, blood-splattered finger at Rebecca.

Obediently, the silver-haired witch crouches over Rebecca and lifts her head, cradling it with one hand while she puts the goblet to her lips.

I fight with every muscle in my body to escape the demon's restraints, silently screaming at Rebecca not to drink. But the silver-haired witch dribbles blood into Rebecca's mouth.

Rebecca splutters, then coughs and gags. Her eyes flick open, and I feel her magic tightening around mine through our coven link. Not that I need anyone else controlling my magic, seeing as the demon already has it locked down.

Rebecca struggles up to sitting, weakly trying to push the silver-haired witch away.

"Drink," snarls the demon. "More!"

A large male witch who must have been watching from behind us rushes forward to hold Rebecca's head still while the silver-haired witch brings the goblet back to her lips.

Rebecca tries to twist her face away, but she's small and weak, and the man has her face locked in his giant hands. Above the goblet, Rebecca's eyes are wild. They focus on me, and I see my own anguish and desperation mirrored there.

The witch forces more blood into her mouth, then clamps one hand over her mouth and nose, so she can't spit it out. Or even breathe, for that matter.

I see Rebecca's throat work as she swallows the blood and the demon's dark magic. In the same moment, there's a tug on the coven link. Rebecca is pulling my magic away from me, yanking it through our link.

My heart clenches and I try desperately to hold my magic back. Will my magic flow out with hers, sucked out by the demon?

As the silver-haired witch pulls the goblet away from Rebecca's lips, Rebecca meets my gaze. Her eyes don't look blank and mindless like the other witches, but urgent, like she's trying to silently tell me something.

With a shock, I understand what she's doing.

She's using the coven link to shield her mind, using our shared magic to protect herself from the demon's control.

I let my magic go, surrendering it to her, letting her pull more away from me. I don't hold back, even when I see tendrils of her white, glowing magic extend from her chest. The demon is taking her magic, like it did to the other witches.

My own magic drains, and I can barely breathe. The effort it takes not to pull back is immense. I feel like she's stripping me bare, leaving me defenceless.

"Now that one," growls Dallas, pointing at Jess.

Behind him, the demon is becoming solid. It's a monstrous creature, black and hairy, with long arms and wicked claws. Its stench of acrid smoke, rotting flesh, and wet dog hair is even stronger now, so foul that I'd do anything to be able to cover my mouth, to stop myself from breathing it in.

The demon is huge, with thick arms and a long pelt. A strong contrast to the frail-looking witch that hosted it. Dallas looks like a walking skeleton. Even his shock of white hair has thinned. But Dallas's eyes still blaze with hate and fury.

The gray-haired witch moves to Jess, lifting the goblet to pour blood down her immobile throat.

The Veritas's eyes go white and a violent wave of magic bursts from her, its shockwave blasting out from her tiny body, like a explosion of pure energy.

The demon's grip on me slips for a moment, and suddenly I can move.

"Go!" screams Rebecca. "Go now!"

I grab Jess, shoving the gray-haired witch aside, and latching onto Jess's arm. Her blood smears over my palm and my dark magic surges, an exhilarating rush of power. I take a staggering step toward Rebecca, so I can grab her as well.

The demon lets out an ear-splitting roar. Its magic rolls out, oozing in a malevolent black wave. It slams Rebecca to the ground, away from me and Jess. Her head smacks the ground with a sick crunch.

Our coven link snaps.

The demon turns to us.

"Go!" I scream the word into Jess's face.

She stares back at me, her eyes huge and her expression terrified.

Then the world disappears.

Chapter Fifteen

I'm freezing.

Apart from Jess, I can't see or hear anything clearly. I don't feel like I'm moving but my vision is so blurred all I can make out are flashes of light. My ears are filled with an unpleasant discordant sound unlike anything I've ever heard. It scratches up and down my spine, making my skin shudder.

My heart clenches, the horror of being a living statue flooding back in a sickening rush. But this isn't the same. Although I can't see or hear anything recognizable, I can move my body, and my hand is still clenched tightly around Jess's arm. She's tugging on my magic, using it through the coven link which is still holding between the two of us, though Rebecca's part of the link has broken away.

Rebecca.

We left her there, wounded and alone. She's just a kid, and she was the one who saved us, rather than the other way around. A hole opens in my chest, and I can't tell if it's from the guilt of leaving Rebecca behind, or the fear of wherever Jess has taken us.

I'm so cold, I'd like to wrap both arms around my body, but there's no way I'm letting go of Jess. I turn my head to her, wanting to speak and not sure if I can.

Jess is glowing.

A faint golden-orange light radiates out from her body. It makes her look like an angel. Am I looking at her power? It doesn't look like the strands of magic I see when I'm using my own magic. But this must be what Jess's time magic looks like.

It's beautiful.

I can't help thinking how amazing Jess's power felt when I cut her and absorbed it. I want to do it again, to feel her magic surge through me. All at once I have to fight a surge of longing so strong, it's all I can do not to dig my fingernails into Jess's skin.

A hard lump rises in my throat. I hate these thoughts. I hate this longing for power, the yearning for blood. I wish I'd never absorbed the dark magic.

Dragging in a deep breath, I turn my face away from Jess's golden glow, staring out into the blurry expanse of swirling, muted color that surrounds us.

Then I see something. A horrible *blackness*, cutting through the blur. The black grows bigger like it's coming closer. As it does, the chill in my bones gets even more intense.

The blackness feels as though it's reaching for me, trying to suck me in.

My skin crawls, and I feel the dark emptiness creep inside me, draining away my life and soul. My gut roils as despairs fill me. I let out a moan, but I can't hear it because the darkness drags it away.

Is this the Nowhere?

Then, with a suddenness that makes my head swim, the discordant noise stops and the darkness changes.

It's still dark, but now it's a warm, friendly kind of dark that's nothing like the freezing, soul-sucking blackness of wherever we just were. We're standing on grass, and the moon is high overhead, spilling cold silver light onto the tall trees that surround us. Jess is shivering next to me, her teeth chattering, and my hand is wrapped so tightly around her arm, I must be hurting her.

"Are you okay?" I ask Jess. My voice sounds weird, probably because my ears still hear a silent echo of that discordant sound. Also because my jaw is clenched so tightly it's hard to talk.

She nods, the movement jerky and convulsive. Then she drags in a shuddering breath. "It wasn't so bad that time," she manages to say.

I swallow. *Not so bad?* "Was that the Nowhere?"

"That? No, I kept us away from the Nowhere. I didn't let it drag us in." A note of pride creeps into her voice.

"Well done." I try to give her a congratulatory smile, but the guilt and grief I feel about having to leave Rebecca behind, combined with the shock of seeing the demon being reborn, and the awful way we got here, probably makes my attempted smile look more like a corpse with rigor mortis.

"Where are we?" I ask.

"We're in the past. I had to take us back in time to get out of there." She's staring at something and when I swivel to face it, I catch a flash of shapes in the distance. People running away. People who look familiar.

"Is that us?" I ask.

She nods. "I pictured where we parked, just after we got out of the car and headed toward the mansion." She drags in a shaky breath, wiping her palms on her jeans as though they're sweaty. "Come on." She strides off in the opposite direction a little way, heading toward the trees.

"Where are you going?" I run to catch up.

She stops on a patch of grass with nothing around. "I can feel the present pulling me back, like Rebecca said. If I bring us back right here, it should be safe." Reaching out, she grabs my hands. "You ready?"

There's no way I want to be dragged back into that freezing, empty nothingness again. But I meet her gaze and give her a nod. "I have less power to give you," I warn.

"I don't think I'll need much," she says, her eyes still glowing with the golden-orange light of her power. "The present is dragging me back. If I can keep us away from the Nowhere, this will be quicker and easier." She hesitates. "I think."

She's right. The second time is much faster, and the blackness doesn't come as close or fill me with such despair. I keep my face averted from Jess, so I'm not tempted by the sight of her power glowing.

When the real world materializes around us, it looks exactly the same as when we left. We're back on the same patch of grass and the night is just as dark.

"Is this the present?" I ask.

The only answer I get is Jess's teeth clattering together. I move closer to her and force my fingers to unlock so I can put my arm around her shoulders. "You okay?"

She nods. "I'm exhausted. That really took it out of me." Her skin feels like ice, and I rub her back, trying to warm her up.

"Car's over there," she says, nodding to the road.

I keep my arm around her as we walk toward it. Xander's waiting by the car, pacing anxiously. Judging from his expression, he's as relieved to see us as I am to see him. He wraps me in a hug and kisses my forehead. "You're freezing," he says. "Where's Rebecca?"

Jess is already getting into the car. "No time for explanations. We need to get out of here."

"She's right." I pull myself reluctantly out of his embrace to get into the passenger seat.

Ratticus is on the dashboard. *"Took your time,"* he grumbles.

Xander starts the car and rolls forward with no lights along the narrow, dark street. I'm expecting him to race away, but he doesn't.

"Can't you go any faster?" I ask.

"Not safely. If I put the headlights on, they'll see us."

So I contain my impatience while we make the slowest getaway in history.

I can only imagine what must be happening behind us, in the council chambers. There's nothing we can do now to stop the demon's transformation. It was close enough to completing it when we got out of there, I have no doubt it'll manage to extract enough power from the rest of the council members to take its full physical form. Rebecca included. My heart lurches, and bile rises up my throat. We left her there to face the demon when we should have been protecting her.

Leaving the park, we turn onto a back street, keeping away from the main expressway. Xander's still driving with the headlights off. The streets are eerily quiet, with no other cars on the road or pedestrians on the sidewalks. The curfew is still in full force.

"Where are we going?" I ask.

"I don't know." Xander shoots me a worried look. "What happened back there?"

"We failed." I close my eyes for a moment, dragging in a deep breath and willing my voice not to crack. "The demon has Rebecca."

"What'll it do to her?"

"It won't kill her." I say it with as much confidence as I

can muster, hoping it's true. "It hasn't killed any of the council, because it's using their power. It's feeding on their magic."

"We shouldn't have gone in there." Jess's voice wavers. "We underestimated the demon."

"*You sure did*," says Ratticus, and I'm glad the others can't hear him.

"We need to get off the street, " says Xander. "There'll be police cars out cruising, looking for anyone breaking the curfew. The further we drive, the more likely we are to get caught."

"Will the demon be looking for us?" asks Jess. "Maybe it won't bother? Not now…?"

I think of the anger and bitterness in Dallas's eyes. "We can't count on that."

"But it didn't need us to create it's physical form," she points out. "Sure, it might have *wanted* our power. But it only *needed* the Veritas."

The demon has its own body now?" Xander's tone is grim. When I nod, he swallows.

"I'm not sure we should go back to Morgan's place," says Jess. "What if it makes her a target? I don't want to drag her into trouble."

"*We need to go back and wait for the smart one*," argues Ratticus. "*She's the only one of you with any sense.*"

"We need to find somewhere close to hole up," says Xander.

"Somewhere we won't get anyone else hurt or killed if it does come after us," adds Jess. Her expression is tight with the same anxious dread I'm feeling.

I stare out the window, my mind racing. This street looks familiar.

Wait.

I recognise this area. I've been here before. To a house

just around the corner. A house that's now empty, its owner dead. Murdered.

It's a house where we could hide out.

More than that, it's a house where there might be information that could help us. Its owner was a dark witch for years, after all. And he studied demons. There could even be a book about Jeqabeel hidden away amongst all his grimoires.

Yeah, it's the perfect place to go. Except for one teensy little problem. I'd rather gulp down a tall glass of warm, chunky vomit than have to walk back into that house. Especially if the Unseen's corpse is still lying in his basement.

Shit.

I swallow hard. I can't believe I'm going to say this. "Turn left here." The words snag in my throat so they come out croaky.

"You know a place we can go?" Xander sounds hopeful as he turns into the street I point to.

I nod wordlessly. As soon as they realize where I'm taking them, Jess and Xander are going to freak out.

"Turn right up ahead," I manage to say. "Then right again at the next intersection."

Xander turns. Driving down the quiet suburban street, I watch the realization slowly dawn on his face.

"No way," he stutters. "No, you can't be serious." He shakes his head and I can see a whole rainbow of other emotions in his expression. Shock. Horror. Anger. Denial. "There must be somewhere else we can go," he insists. "Anywhere but there."

"What's wrong?" Jess is looking confused. "Where are you taking us?"

"Somewhere bad," says Xander. I can tell he's wracking his brain for any other option, just like I did.

Finally, like me, he gets a look of resignation and reluctant acceptance. "But I guess there's nowhere else."

"On the bright side, Aunt Therese said the Unseen was obsessed by demon dimensions," I tell him. "He researched them for years. Which means we might find something useful at his house."

"The Unseen's house?" Jess jerks forward in her seat, her eyes wide with horror. "Are you high? I'm never stepping foot in that place again."

"*Me neither.*" Ratticus scrambles up my clothing, onto my shoulder.

"We could find answers there," I say. "The Unseen had a thing for Jeqabeel. For all we know, he could have left instructions on how to banish the demon tacked to his wall." I'm trying to sound convincing, but the memories of Jess being tortured and Xander lying dead on the floor are all too vivid.

"Nobody will think to look for us there," agrees Xander. "It's as safe as anywhere."

"*Not as safe as the smart one's house.*" Ratticus sounds wistful.

In the back seat, Jess tightens her mouth, staring out the side window. She looks as sick as I feel, and doesn't say another word until we park outside a familiar bungalow.

Even at night, it's so sweet looking, I'm in danger of developing a spontaneous case of diabetes. The house is lit up by both the street lights, and some ornamental lamps that line the path to the front door. They twinkle prettily, illuminating a pair of garden gnomes fishing in an ornamental pond in the front garden and roses flowering along the cute picket fence. The mat in front of the door reads *Home Sweet Home.*

"Welcome to hell," mutters Jess. "Wipe your feet on your way inside."

Chapter Sixteen

s soon as I open the car door, my lungs fill with the sickly smell of roses. The night is dark and quiet, and the smell gets even stronger as I walk up to the front door with Ratticus still on my shoulder.

The Unseen's magical wards don't snag me on my way up the path. They're not there anymore. Of course they're not. I killed the Unseen in the most gruesome way possible, by yanking his heart right out of his chest. With nobody left to protect, his wards must have dissolved.

My hand tingles as I remember the feel of the Unseen's beating heart in my palm. I swallow a wave of nausea at the memory, but at the same time I feel a rush of longing for the power his murder gave me. My dark magic uncurls inside me, a fuse waiting to be lit.

"You okay?" asks Xander, catching up to me. "You look pale."

I shake my head, trying to banish all memories of what happened here as I step outside the front door. "I'm fine. Just wondering if the Unseen's body is still here, in his basement."

Xander stops beside me. "I doubt it. Your friend Magnus said he was going to deal with it, whatever that means." He tries the door handle and clicks his tongue. "Dammit. It's locked."

"Do you have your lock pickers?" I ask, wondering if I have enough magic left in me to open it. But Jess is already moving around the side of the house. A moment later, I hear glass smash. When I follow her around the corner, Jess is half-hidden in the shadows, but I can see her dark form kicking in a window more fiercely than is strictly necessary to get us inside.

"I'll go in first," I say when she finally stops kicking. "In case there are any magical boobytraps." Before Xander can protest, I duck through the broken window.

I wish I had a flashlight. As many times as I've been in the Unseen's basement, I've never seen the rest of the house, so I have no idea what kind of room this is, only that it smells musty and dank. My boots stick unpleasantly to the carpet as I feel my way along a wall, searching for a light switch. When I finally find one, it's for a dim lamp in the corner, but the weak light reveals a small, gloomy room decorated with old couches, a dusty bookcase, pictures of hideous monsters on the walls, and a thick layer of grime over everything. It's a living room, I guess, if it's possible to call a room that when nobody in their right mind would want to live in it.

I walk through the room to the hallway, and turn on as many light switches as I can find. From the hall, I can look down to the front door, and see the door that leads into the basement. Ignoring it, I peer into the kitchen. Dirty dishes litter the counter, and two large cockroaches sit on the wall waving their feelers, presumably waiting to see if I'm a threat before they decide whether to bother fleeing.

The Unseen was misnamed. He should have been called the *Unclean*.

At least I haven't felt any tingles of magic. Whatever protections the Unseen had in place must have died when he did.

There are three more doors, and I stick my head into a bedroom that contains an unmade bed, a pile of dirty clothing heaped on a dresser, and the pungent stench of stale body odour. One glance at the bathroom next to it is enough to make me gag and back away, though I leave the light turned on in there. There's another tiny room with a bed that doesn't smell quite as bad, but it has a layer of dust so thick I'm not entirely certain whether the bedspread is supposed to be gray, or if it's filthy.

Finally, I stop at the doorway to the basement, and force myself to glance down the black stairwell, though I can't see a thing. Now I'm getting tingles. But it's not a magical booby trap that's causing the sensation. It's all the blood that's been spilled down there.

Jess's blood. Xander's blood. The Unseen's blood. All of it taken by force, with pain and suffering. And some of that pain and suffering was inflicted by me.

The thought of it makes me sick, but my dark magic is surging, filling me with longing. A hungry voice whispers inside me, reminding me that blood is power, and I'll need all the power I can get to have any hope against the demon…

"No," I mutter out loud. "I'm not going down there."

"At least you have that much sense," mutters Ratticus. *"I was about to put together a search party to hunt for your brain."*

Gritting my teeth, I retreat back to the living room, where Jess and Xander are waiting outside the broken window. "It's safe," I call to them. "Well, relatively safe. As long as you're up to date on your tetanus shots." On the wall in the living room, I find another light switch and flick it on. The main ceiling light comes on, and in the sudden brightness, the pictures on the walls look even creepier.

Most are crude drawings of monsters. Demons, I guess, of all shapes and sizes. Some are hairy, some are scaly, some covered with horns, or spikes, or bristles. The drawings are pinned to the wall like a teenager's posters of their favorite band.

Xander moves next to me. "There's Jeqabeel." He points to one of the drawings. "Any idea what the other ones are?"

I shrug. "The ugliest boy band in the universe?"

"Check out that picture." Jess points to a drawing that my gaze doesn't want to settle on. It's a complicated arrangement of symbols that makes my eyes try to cross and my skin crawl.

"What the hell is it?" asks Xander. He turns away, blinking. "Actually, I don't want to know. It's only lines on paper, but looking at it makes me want to scrub my eyeballs."

"Aunt Therese was right about the Unseen being obsessed with demons," I muse. "Whatever that drawing is, it's not from this dimension."

"Is there any food in the kitchen?" Jess is already heading into the hallway and I follow, mainly to get away from the Unseen's twisted idea of artwork. It's well after midnight, but we haven't eaten for several hours, and I'm not surprised Jess is hungry after using her magic.

The cockroaches are still on the kitchen wall, holding their ground. Jess screws up her nose, but starts opening cupboards. "I'm too hungry to worry about the filth," she says. "Even going back in time for a few minutes takes a lot of—Aha!" She tugs out a box of cereal. "This hasn't been opened yet."

She rips open the box, then the pouch inside, and reaches in to grab a handful of the dry flakes. With her mouth full, she offers the box to me. "Ya wan' some?"

"Thanks." I take some of the flakes and crunch them. It's not exactly cordon bleu cuisine, but my stomach is rumbling too.

"*What about me?*"

"Here." I hand a cornflake to Ratticus and he sits up on my shoulder to eat it.

"There are some cans in there." Jess nods at the still-open cupboard. "I could sterilize a pot and throw together some kind of stew."

"*I like stew.*" Weirdly, although Ratticus is only speaking in my head, it sounds like he's mumbling the words through a mouthful of cereal.

I cast a doubtful look at the grease splatters that cover the stove, but Jess sets to work filling the sink with hot water and squeezing in plenty of detergent.

"You want some help?" I ask half-heartedly.

She shakes her head. "I've got this. You go find something we can use to get Rebecca back. Preferably something that'll kill the demon."

"It's immortal. It can't be killed."

She waves a wet hand. "Something to hurt it, then. I'll take whatever we can get."

I head back into the living room, where Xander is examining the books stacked in the dusty bookcase.

"What about these?" he asks. "This book has a black cover."

I frown at it, then shake my head. "None of these books feel powerful. Not like the grimoires in the basement." I frown at the book he's pointing to, straining my eyes to read the faded title. "Wait." My voice rises incredulously. "Is that a copy of *Twilight*?"

"A copy of what?" Xander gives me a confused look.

"The sparkly vampire book." I shake my head. "Never mind. It's not exactly what I expected to find in the Unseen's bookcase, is all."

"What did you expect?

"I don't know. But I'd like to find a book called, *How To Banish a Jackal Demon Back to its Own Dimension*. You think he's got one like that?"

"Yup. Here it is." Xander pulls out a slim volume. "*Dealing With Dangerous Pets*. Close enough, right?"

"I dare you to say that to the demon's face."

Xander grimaces, and I shoot him the best smile I can manage, given the circumstances.

When I return to the bookshelf, I notice a small bound hardback. I pick it up, flicking through the pages. It's just a mundane zoology book, but something about the binding reminds me of the book I found in Sylvia's athenaeum, the one with the *Binde Magick* spell that helped me absorb spells. The one that was dedicated to someone with my name.

What was that dedication again?

I reach inside me for the words, and find them with the book's spells.

This book is dedicated to Sapphira. Follow the strands, no matter how tangled, to the beginning of the skein.

Bringing it up on my arm, I read the words again as they run over my skin. Everything else in the book has been useful, but I haven't figured out what the dedication means.

"What's that?" Xander steps closer to peer at my arm. "Oh wait. It's the dedication from that book you found at Sylvia's place, right?"

I nod. "This book had the spell that allowed me to absorb the dark magic. And it had a section about

Jeqabeel." When his gaze sharpens, I add, "But it was written over a century ago. Who knows how many people called Sapphira were wandering around back then? Could have been the most common name in Maryland."

"Still, it seems like a pretty big coincidence."

"Dinner's cooking. Shouldn't be too long." Jess steps into the room and frowns at my arm. "Is that a clue?"

"Maybe. But I don't know what it means." I hesitate, thinking it over. "Whenever I see magic, it always looks like strands. And my magic used to get tangled all the time." I let out a frustrated breath. "But even if I'm on the right track, I still have no clue what it's trying to tell me, or how to follow the strands."

Jess grunts, staring at the dedication. "What if it's talking about time? Rebecca said time was like strands of yarn. Maybe the demon being here is like the strands being tangled."

"Maybe," I say doubtfully. "I guess it's easier to follow time back to the beginning, at least for you. But where *is* the beginning of the skein?"

"It might be trying to tell us that Jess could use her magic to fix everything." Xander sounds hopeful. "What if she could go back in time and throw the bone into the sea before the demon ever manages to get out of it?"

I shake my head. "What if she throws it out to sea and it washes up on shore? It'd possess the first person to pick it up. It might even get out faster."

"I could bury it in a deep hole where nobody will ever find it," Jess suggests.

"Unless a house gets built in that spot, or it gets pushed to the surface by tree roots." I tap my finger against my lip, wondering if we're onto something, and this could be a way to fight back. "Whatever we come up with needs to be foolproof. The bone was sealed in a case, locked in a safe, guarded by witches. Somehow the demon still managed to get free."

"If we put our heads together, I'm sure we could come up with something." Xander sounds hopeful. "Imagine if Jess could go back and make it so Jeqabeel can't get out. None of this will have ever happened. Everything could change."

The idea is tantilizing. If the demon hadn't been set free, my parents would still be alive. The last five years of my life would be totally different. The loneliness, the fear, the grief. All of it gone.

"But what if I mess up the timeline and kill everyone?" Jess shakes her head. "Rebecca thought it was too dangerous, and she knew more about my power than any of us."

"We could look for books on time travel," suggests Xander. "The Unseen has so many, maybe he'll have one that can help Jess understand her power."

We all turn back to the bookcase to scan the volumes. "Nothing here," I announce after a few minutes.

"I'd better go and stir the stew before it burns." Jess disappears back into the kitchen.

"What about the books in the basement?" asks Xander. "We might find something down there."

"*Demon dude is crazy.*" Ratticus burrows into the neck of my shirt, making me twitch. "*Don't listen to him. I don't want to go back down there.*"

As much as I agree with Ratticus, Xander is right. We can't afford not to look everywhere for help.

"The Unseen kept his dark magic grimoires downstairs," I say. "So we're more likely to find something helpful there."

"*Why aren't you listening to me?*" Ratticus chitters in my head.

Xander's already moving to the stairwell. "You think

we can find a light switch this time? I didn't like when he made us walk down in the dark." He searches the walls. "What's this?" The narrow stairwell floods with light. "There. That was easy."

He turns to me with a satisfied look, and I have to admit the stairwell looks a lot less creepy than before, though the scent and pull of the blood down there is still as strong as ever. On the plus side, at least I can't smell the foul stench of a rotting corpse, so Xander must have been right about Magnus removing the Unseen's body.

Xander takes the steps quickly, disappearing into the basement. Dragging in a few more deep breaths, I follow more slowly, telling myself the lure of all that blood won't be a big deal. I can handle it. I can control my dark magic enough to not let myself touch it.

"*I'm going to need that search party after all.*" Ratticus nips my ear lobe. Hard.

"Ouch." I push him away from my face. "Don't worry, Cowardus. The Unseen's dead, remember? The only thing down here that can hurt you is me." I lower my voice into a snarl. "So no more biting, okay?"

"*I'll stop biting when you stop doing dumb things. Like walking into dangerous places.*"

"It's not dangerous anymore. Look." Reaching the bottom of the stairwell, I motion to the ripped-up stone floor, the toppled bookcases, and the grimoires scattered on the ground. I'm trying not to stare at the bloodstains, but I can taste blood in the back of my throat, and my dark magic is humming like the Handel Choir. Just one touch and it would burst into song.

I clench my fists and shove them in the pockets of my jeans. It's a tight fit, which is a good thing. The tighter they're held, the better.

"Did you say something?" asks Xander. He's picked a grimoire off the floor and is flipping through it.

"Nothing important." Now's not the time to try to explain about Ratticus speaking into my head.

"This book is blank." Xander drops the grimoire with a frown. Then he steps over to one of the few bookcases in the room that's still standing, its contents intact. "We should check these books. And the other junk on the shelves." He picks up a jar filled with a cloudy liquid, with something solid and fleshy sloshing inside it. "What do you suppose this might be?"

I force myself to walk carefully over to him, stepping around all major bloodstains. "Eye of newt, perhaps?" I force my voice to stay light, to give no hint of the struggle going on between my longing for power and my revulsion for the dark magic inside me. "Or the dissected body of an annoying rat?"

I lift my hands, expecting to have to fend off another bite, but Ratticus is sitting motionless on my shoulder, whiskers twitching, staring to the far side of the large basement, where the bookcase toppled over and fell on me, and I absorbed its grimoires.

"*There's something there.*" His reedy voice gets even higher. "*Magic powerful enough to ruffle my fur. You were wrong about this place not being dangerous. What a surprise.*"

I can't feel any magic, but then again, the pull of the blood is so strong, it's hard to concentrate on anything else. When I step closer to where he's looking, Ratticus gives a startled squeak. "*Don't go near it, stupid. That was a warning, not an invitation.*"

"Wait here." I put him down on the shelf where he scuttles behind the jar, trying to squash his plump body into the small space behind it.

"Why? What is it?" asks Xander. He must think I was talking to him, because he doesn't follow me.

"I'm not sure yet. Some kind of magic." Walking toward the fallen bookcase, I concentrate on shutting out the pull of the blood, searching for a different kind of magic. Ratticus is right, there's something there. A buzzing at the edge of my senses. Dark magic.

One of the Unseen's spells must have survived his death.

Though I can't see anything unusual, the sensation leads me to the innocent-looking wall behind the toppled bookcase.

"Be careful, Saffy." Xander sounds tense. "I can't imagine the Unseen leaving behind any pleasant surprises."

"Whatever it is, he didn't want anyone to find it." To reach the right spot, I have to crawl over the back of the fallen bookcase, forcing my way through a magic barrier that's so subtly woven, I can barely feel it pushing me away. With difficulty, I manage to stretch my hand out to touch the wall. Though it still looks ordinary, like it's made from the same old, stained wood as the rest of the basement, my fingers catch on a lever that I can feel, but not see.

"How are you doing that?" asks Xander. "It looks like you're pushing your hand through the wall."

I fumble with the lever, my eyes crossing at the weird sight of my hand appearing to sink into the wood. The lever doesn't budge, but starts to heat up. The more I try to move the lever, pushing and pulling it to try to activate whatever it's hiding, the warmer it gets.

Eventually, I have to let it go. "Dammit." I suck my singed fingers. "That hurt."

"Are you okay?" Xander crosses to me. "What is it?"

"The Unseen left magical wards to protect something

in this wall." I nod at the spot. "The bookcase must have been in front of it, too. So whatever it is was physically hidden as well as warded."

Xander frowns. "What would be important enough for the Unseen to keep so well protected? Maybe something he didn't want the council to find?"

I shake my head. "He probably wasn't hiding it from the council. If they got into this room, they'd know he was using dark magic just by looking at his grimoires. That would be enough for them to turn him into stone, and that's their worst punishment."

"Then maybe it's something he didn't want *Jequabeel* to know he had."

"Maybe," I agree slowly. It feels like maybe we're jumping to conclusions that we want to be true. But it does make sense. Perhaps before bringing the demon here, the Unseen hid something from it.

Excitement rises inside me, though I try to convince myself not to get my hopes up. Xander's cheeks are flushed and his ice blue eyes have a hopeful glint. "Could it be an insurance policy?" he breathes. "Some way he thought he could control the demon in case things went wrong?"

"Let's not get ahead of ourselves," I warn. "If the Unseen went to all this trouble to hide his postage stamp collection, we're both going to be crushed."

"Can you get rid of his wards?" Xander asks.

"They're dark magic wards." I swallow, looking at the bloodstains on the floor. "I'll have to use dark magic to dissolve them."

"Is that a good idea?" He looks at me with a serious expression, and I know he's thinking about how I woke up standing over Jess, knife in hand.

He's right, but with so much at stake, I can't afford to be squeamish. Every time I use the dark magic, it'll grow stronger inside me and harder to control. But what choice do I have?

"I'll be fine," I say, trying to sound off-hand. "Not a problem."

Except, as I walk toward the bloodstains on the floor, there's a definite problem, namely the way my hands tremble with anticipation and my heart hammers faster than a room full of carpenters.

My dark magic feels like the most amazing present in the world that I'm finally getting to open. It also feels like a scary, revolting curse, but only in an intellectual way. Every part of me but my brain is celebrating.

It's wrong.

It feels so right.

The large bloodstain on the floor came from Jess's torture, from the Unseen's murder, from Xander having the demon's symbol carved into his chest. But bending to put my hands on the darkened stones, my only misgivings are because I'm wishing the blood were still wet. If only it were fresh, it would be far more potent. As it is, it barely powers my dark magic, barely brings it to life.

But what little power the blood-soaked stone gives me feels so good, I have to suppress a groan, and close my eyes for a moment to savor the feeling.

"You okay, Saff?" asks Xander, his voice concerned. He clearly didn't believe my assurances that I was fine.

But I force myself to nod and straighten, then turn back to the fallen bookcase. With the dark magic humming inside me, I can see the strands of the Unseen's red magic stretched like a spider's web across a cavity in the wall. Inside the cavity is a metal safe with an impressive combination lock.

Striding over to it, I make the stone floor ripple like ocean waves to push the bookcase aside. Then I thrust my hand through the spider's web of magic, using my earth magic to soften the metal front of the safe, melting the combination lock so I can pull it away.

The Unseen's glamor dissolves as the door of the safe flies open.

A shockwave radiates out from inside the safe, slamming me backward. I land hard on the ground, the wind knocked out of me.

Xander lets out a grunt of pain and I whip my head around, searching for him. "Xander?"

"I'm okay." He picks himself up from the ground and steps over to help me up. "What was that?"

"*Something best left alone*," mutters Ratticus.

I stand on shaky legs and stare over at the safe.

There's an object inside it.

Chapter Seventeen

The thing in the safe is white and gives me the same weird, dizzy feeling as the drawing on the wall upstairs.

"It has a repelling spell on it," I tell Xander. "The strongest one I've ever felt." The spell is still active, because I can feel it pushing against me, keeping me away from whatever the thing in the safe is.

"Can you override it?" he asks.

I stand up and take a step toward it, reaching out with my dark magic. The object slams me back.

"Doesn't seem like I can," I tell him.

"Shit."

"Dinner's ready." It's Jess's voice, calling from the top of the stairs. "Are you in the basement? In the middle of the night?" A moment later, she comes into view peering down at us. "Did you find a book on time travel?"

"Not yet. But we found something else."

Jess wrinkles her nose. "Let me guess. Something gross and disgusting?" She comes further down the steps into the basement anyway.

"We found that." I motion to the thing in the safe. "But we're not sure what it is, and we can't get close enough to…" My voice trails away as Jess walks over to the safe, peers into it, then reaches in and draws out the object inside.

Xander gapes at her, looking as shocked as I feel. "You can touch it?" he asks. It's a redundant question seeing as she's already holding it, but I refrain from pointing that out.

Ratticus isn't so polite. *"A brilliant deduction. I can see why he's a detective."*

"What do you mean?" Jess frowns at Xander. "You can't touch it?"

She takes a step toward us, and the repelling spell shoves me away, so I have to step backward. Xander steps back at the same time, so he's obviously affected like I am.

"Don't bring it any closer," I warn Jess. "Neither of us can get near it."

But even as I say it, the repelling spell seems to be weakening. The push against me is lessening, as though Jess is somehow draining the spell's power.

"It feels weird. Unpleasant." Jess peers at the object, her mouth twisted with distaste. "It feels like it's vibrating, but not in a good way. What is it, anyway? I mean, it's obviously a pentagramic antiprism. But what's it *for*?"

My mouth drops open. "Um." I say stupidly. "It's a what?"

She gives me a 'duh' look. "A pentagramic antiprism. It's basically a three dimensional pentagram."

I blink at her. Jess is full of surprises. How on earth does a drummer—with a side job of stripping the parts from stolen cars—know what a pentagramic what-ever-she-said is?

Even though I don't ask the question aloud, she must

see it written on my face. "One of my favorite heavy metal bands uses it as a symbol," she explains. "It's on all their album covers, and I was curious, so I looked it up."

"It doesn't hurt your brain to look at it?" asks Xander.

"Of course not. Why would it? It's just a geometric shape." She holds it up to give us both a better look, and I squint at it, trying to get the sides to stop warping. It reminds me of one of those brain twister puzzles where your eyes can be tricked into seeing two completely different pictures.

"I don't like holding it," Jess adds. "It gives me the creeps." She moves to put it down, but Xander holds up a hand to stop her.

"Does it feel solid, or hollow?" he asks.

"Definitely solid." She weighs it in her hands. "It's as heavy as a rock, but I'm pretty sure it's been carved out of bone. Maybe a fossilized dinosaur bone, or something much bigger and heavier than any human bone."

"You think there could be something inside it?" I suggest.

Jess shrugs and puts the object down. "Anyway, I came to tell you that dinner's ready." She walks toward the stairs. "Come and eat, before it gets cold."

"*I'm starving,*" says Ratticus. "*Stop messing around and let's go.*"

Xander and I exchange a look. Though the spell seems to be slowly wearing off, I still can't get close enough to the object to touch it.

So how come Jess could?

"I guess we can figure this out after dinner," says Xander.

"*That's the smartest thing demon-dude has ever said,*" agrees Ratticus.

I collect Ratticus from the bookcase, putting him back

on my shoulder, and follow Xander upstairs. But instead of going to the kitchen, where Jess is already ladling out steaming bowls of stew, Xander and I head back to the living room. We don't even need to talk about it, we just both go and stand in front of the weird, mind-bending drawing in the living room.

"*What are you doing?*" demands Ratticus. "*It's time to eat, remember?*"

I pluck him off my shoulder and put him on the floor. "Go and hassle Jess. I'm sure she'll feed you." He gives an indignant squeak, but hurries off.

"That drawing looks like the thing in the safe," Xander says when I straighten. "A three-dimensional pentagram. But what's it for?"

"Look." I point to another drawing that's pinned next to the pentagram. It's a black-and-white sketch of an ugly, animal-like demon, with stocky legs and a massive head. Its enormous fangs protrude from an oversized mouth, reminding me of the hideous deep-sea angler fish from *Finding Nemo*. Sketched over the demon's chest, difficult to spot, is an image of the pentagram. And though I scan the other demon drawings, looking for the image, I can't see it anywhere else.

"You think that pentagram thing could have been carved from bone that came from the chest of a demon?" I ask.

Xander studies the drawing, then gives a slow nod. "Maybe. We can't know for sure, but the theory's no weirder than anything else that's happened."

"Why would the Unseen keep something like that locked away?" I ask.

"It might be something to do with time travel. That would explain why Jess could pick it up, if it has something to do with her power."

"We thought it could be some kind of insurance policy," I say. "Maybe the Unseen was planning to travel back in time if the demon turned on him. The pentagram bone could be an artefact that would help him do it."

Xander shrugs. "How will we know? Unless we find written instructions for it, we're just guessing."

"You coming?" interrupts Jess, sticking her head into the living room. "Not to complain, but I've been sweating over a hot stove, and Ratticus just tried to climb into the pot I cooked the stew in. I think he was planning to swim around in it."

"Be right there." I rub my stomach, which has started to rumble.

"Tomorrow, we should take a good look through everything," Xander says as we head into the kitchen. "Maybe we'll get lucky and find those instructions."

"Sure." I sit at the freshly-wiped table in the small dining nook off the kitchen, where steaming bowls of stew are waiting for us. "But I still think going back in time and getting rid of the bone from my mother's safe is the only way we're going to fix this." I can't help but dream about being able to change everything that way, and bring my parents back to life.

Jess shakes her head, sitting opposite me. "Not unless we can find out how time travel works. I don't want to try and make things better in the past, and get back to the present to find I've wiped out the entire human race, and the planet's been overrun with talking animals."

"*Sounds okay to me,*" says Ratticus. "*As long as there's still pizza.*" He's on the floor, tucking into a small plate of stew of his own.

Xander picks up his fork. He's wearing his detective expression. "There's nobody who could teach you what you can and can't do? How do witches normally learn about their magic?"

"Usually from a parent," Jess says. "Magic runs in families. But my mother was the only one in our family with the same kind of power, and she disappeared when I was six."

I'm about to take a bite of stew, but I freeze with my fork at my lips as a thought occurs to me. "Why can't you go back in time and ask her to teach you?"

Jess's eyes go wide. Both Xander and I lower our forks, our stew forgotten, as the idea sinks in. Jess's mouth opens and closes again. She swallows. "Go back in time and see my mother?" Her voice is hoarse and her expression is cycling between fear and hope.

Xander looks at me, then at Jess. "It makes sense."

"But… could I even do that?" she asks.

"I don't know," I say. "Could you?"

Chapter Eighteen

W e all eventually eat Jess's stew, but I don't think any of us actually taste it. We're too keyed up by the possibility that Jess might be able to get help from her mother.

Well, Xander and I are excited. Jess is reluctant.

"I can't go back that far." She toys with her food, stirring it with her fork.

"I bet you can," I tell her. "The Veritas said you need to use a really strong memory, and you vividly remember the day your mother disappeared. You told me about it. "

She shakes her head. "It's too dangerous. The same level of danger as if I went back to get rid of the bone with the demon in it. '

"No, it's not. This way you wouldn't change anything in the past, except for talking to your mother. How could that hurt the timeline?" I'm pushing pretty hard, but if Jess can learn to use her power, she could solve all our problems.

I can't stop thinking about the blood in the basement,

and I have to try hard not to sound impatient. It feels like my skin is stretched a little too tight.

"The risk is lower," agrees Xander. "If your mother thinks it's dangerous, she can send you right back."

"By then it could be too late." Jess's jaw is set. "The damage could be done."

"Can you think of any other way to stop the demon?" I'm trying to sound reasonable and patient, but I can't believe she's objecting. If our positions were reversed, I'd risk anything to see my mother again, let alone grabbing hold of our only chance to stop Jeqabeel.

"It's your lives I'm putting in danger," she points out.

I shrug. "The likelihood of the demon killing everyone in Baltimore is getting higher by the minute. We're pretty much doomed anyway. At least this way we'd have a chance."

She scrunches up her face. "That's real comforting, Saff."

"I'd rather be killed by you than the demon." I nudge Xander to back me up. "Wouldn't you?"

He frowns, and swallows his last mouthful of stew. "Are those my only two choices?"

"Unless Jess saves us all."

"I choose that option." He catches my pointed look. "But if it happens to go terribly wrong, death by Jess is the next best thing. Wouldn't want to die any other way."

"It'd be a long jump to get back that far." Jess is spending more time chewing on her lip than she is finishing what's left of her stew. "What if I can't make it? I could get stuck in the Nowhere."

I think of the black nothingness of time travel, and repress a shudder. "I'll go with you, to feed you my power." As much as the thought scares me, I can't let her go alone. "No matter where we end up, you know how to bring us back to this time." I put my hand on her arm and give her a reassuring smile. "You've got this, Jess. We believe in you, and I'll be with you all the way."

Xander clears his throat. "Maybe instead of leaping straight into it, you could practice going back in shorter increments?"

I shake my head. "If she exhausts herself doing that, she won't be able to make a bigger jump. We don't have time for Jess to try shorter jumps and have to recover."

"But the only jump I've ever done on purpose was the one to get us out of the council chambers."

"That one went well, didn't it?" I try to sound upbeat.

Jess drags in a deep breath, and I can see her wavering.

"You won't be alone," I tell her. "I'll be with you."

She purses her lips. "But what if you go with me and neither of us make it back? You should stay here. If something bad happens to me, you and Xander need to keep fighting the demon."

Xander grimaces. "And I don't have any magical powers to fight it with."

"You're forgetting the Veritas's vision," I say. "I was helping the demon, remember?"

Jess shakes her head. "I don't believe you'd do that."

"Neither do I." Xander leans across the table to touch my hand. "I know this magic you absorbed is bad stuff, but there's no way you'd give into it. Anyone who thinks that doesn't know you at all."

I give him a grateful smile. "Thanks. But Jess, you'll need my power to jump so far back in time."

"You could cut yourself before I go, and push all your power to me through our coven link."

"But then you'd be on your own, and—"

"Believe it or not, I'd feel better about doing it that way." She meets my gaze, her tone firm. "My biggest fear

—after ending up in the Nowhere—is accidentally changing something and destroying the present. If you're with me, that's double the chance of making a mistake."

"But I'd be careful."

"I go alone or not at all." She gives me an apologetic shrug. "No offense, but it's dangerous enough without adding extra risk."

"So you'll do it?" asks Xander.

"I don't know. I'll sleep on it." Jess rubs her eyes. "What time is it? The adrenaline must be wearing off, because I really want to lie down."

"Me too." Xander yawns. "Where are we going to sleep?"

"There's a bed in the spare room, and the couch in the living room," I say. I glance toward the hallway. "There's the Unseen's bedroom as well…"

Xander makes a face as he stands up. "I don't think anyone should go near the Unseen's room. It's a bio-hazard. You two share the spare bed, and I'll take the couch."

We clean up the dishes, then Jess and I head to the second bedroom. I open the window to let in some fresh air, and Jess pulls off the dust-covered bedspread.

"I think I saw a clean blanket in the back of the car." says Jess, sneezing. "We can sleep on top of that."

When we're finished, the bedroom is still musty, but I'm too tired to care.

I fall asleep as soon as I lie down, and wake up feeling groggy, like I could easily sleep for another week. Sun is filtering in the bedroom, but it feels early and I doubt I've slept more than four or five hours. Jess and Xander are already up, and I can hear them talking in the kitchen.

After washing in the disgusting bathroom, I head into the kitchen to join them.

"When it comes down to it, I don't see that I have a choice." I hear Jess say as I approach.

"Let's not decide yet," says Xander. "First, let's search this place for books about time travel. If we can find more information, you won't have to risk it."

Jess nods, but when she turns to me, I see something other than fear in her eyes. Maybe she dreamed she got to see her mother again. Perhaps it's just that she's slept, the morning is bright, and she's in the mood to try something crazy. Whatever the reason, last night's fear has turned to eagerness.

"Morning," I say. "What am I missing?"

"*Not much to eat around here.*" Ratticus sounds as grumpy as ever. He's sitting on one of the kitchen chairs, nibbling on a cracker.

"We're about to search all the Unseen's books." Xander says, handing me the box of dry cereal. "Want some breakfast before we start?"

"Thanks." I crunch a mouthful. "We're going back to the basement?"

Xander nods. "Jess and I already went through every one of the books up here. We didn't find anything helpful."

"You need to look at the dark magic grimoires, Saff." Jess wrinkles her nose. "Xander and I won't be able to read them, and it's dangerous for us to touch them."

"Okay," I mumble, trying not to spray dry cereal as I talk. I keep my face down, pretending to study the side of the cereal box so they can't see my enthusiasm for the idea. "The quickest way to do it would be for me to absorb the spells from the grimoires."

"Absorb more dark magic?" Jess shakes her head. "No way. Absolutely not."

"If we're going to have any chance against Jeqabeel, I'll need as much power as I can get."

"You're already too close to the edge of your control, Saff. Remember the other night?" Jess's expression is stern.

"I'm with Jess," says Xander. "Yesterday in the basement, you didn't seem fine. And if the dark magic is what made you pick up that knife the other night—"

"I need the power," I snap. Then I drag in a breath, trying to calm my flash of anger. "It'd be silly to waste it." I make an effort to sound reasonable, resisting the urge to remind them that neither of them could stop me if I decided to just take it.

Jess folds her arms, her expression dark. "You want to turn into the Unseen? To become evil, and blood thirsty, and… and stinky?"

I let out a derisive snort. "You're exaggerating. I won't become—"

"Yes, you *will*." She glowers at me. "You're just saying you won't because the magic is already changing you."

"She's right." Xander puts his hand on my arm, his voice gentle. "This isn't you, Saff. Even since you used the dark magic again yesterday, you've been a little off. I'm afraid for you."

The concern in his eyes is like a splash of cold water on my face that clears my fog of hunger for the dark magic.

Putting the cereal box down, I wipe my hands on my jeans as I turn away. "Okay. I won't absorb any more grimoires." My voice comes out thin and weak. They're right. The dark magic is changing me. And though it's probably already too late to stop it, there's no reason to hurry it along, no matter how incredible the power feels.

"I'll look through the grimoires to check for anything to do with time magic or dealing with demons. That's all." Without waiting for them to agree, I lead the way to the basement. The weird pentagram thing is still there, waiting for me to inspect it, but now all I want to do is get this nightmare over with. Having to handle the books without absorbing their magic is going to be hard enough, especially in the basement surrounded by blood. If I don't finish the job fast, I might not be able to resist breaking my promise and absorbing more of the power I crave.

When I stop in front of the bookcase, Xander is close beside me. "You okay?" he asks softly.

"I will be." Pulling out one of the grimoires, I quickly flip through it. This way I don't need to look at him, to see the worry on his face. To know he's imagining the dark magic taking control of me.

"Okay." He puts one hand on my back, rubbing circles. "Let me know if I can help."

"Sure." It takes everything I have to keep my tone light, but somehow I manage it. In my hands, the grimoire pulses with raw, seductive power. To put it back on the shelf and take out the next one is a feat Hercules would have been proud of.

Xander strokes my back with one last circle, then leaves me to the job. While he and Jess examine all the jars and bottles and other containers of gross things displayed on the Unseen's shelves, I open each grimoire in turn, scanning its contents. Fighting the magic's siren call.

It sucks.

Badly.

The only thing that keeps me going, keeps me fighting the urge to absorb the spells, is the watchful presence of Jess and Xander. They're pretending not to be keeping a sharp eye on me. But I can feel the weight of their gaze, and read the worry in their faces.

Finally, after an endless eternity of torment that's almost as bad as spending all that time as a statue, I slide the last grimoire back into the bookcase, shove my shaking hands in my pockets, and turn to the others.

I have to clear my throat to make my voice work. "There was nothing in the grimoires about time magic," I say. "Or about Jeqabeel. Or that pentagramic thing." I manage a shrug that I hope comes off as relaxed. Or, at least like I'm not in agony, fighting not to break down and devour every last dark magic spell in here. "Nothing useful at all." I feel like I'm sweating on the inside of my skin. Like my internal organs are perspiring.

"We couldn't find anything either," says Jess.

Now the repelling spell has completely worn off, I can walk over and pick up the pentagram bone. Jess was right about it being heavy. It feels like I'm carrying a bowling ball, but instead of being lifeless in my hands, it has a weird kind of energy. It has *power*. A little like the dark magic grimoires do, only it feels different. Even darker, if that's possible.

"Let's go back upstairs. Maybe we can figure out what this thing does." I'm both relieved and desperately sorry to climb the stairs out of the basement. At least in the Unseen's living room, some fresh air is coming in through the broken window. I breathe it in deeply, moving to stand in front of the empty window frame. The pentagramic antiprism is getting heavier and heavier, as though it wants me to put it down. And I'm happy to oblige. I place it carefully on one of the bookcase's shelves, next to the Unseen's copy of *Twilight*.

"I guess our decision's made," says Jess. "Now our only remaining plan is for me to go back in time and talk to my mother."

"I still think it's a bad idea for you to risk going alone," I tell her. Maybe it's wrong to put so much on Jess's shoulders, but without her, we'd be at a dead end. "You sure you don't want me to come?"

"I'm sure." She drags in a breath, but she still seems

more eager than afraid. "I guess I should just go, right? The sooner the better."

She goes to the kitchen and rummages in the drawer until she finds a couple of sharp knives. "You give me your power, Saff. Then I'll cut myself, and travel."

I nod. "If I cut myself, I can give you my normal magic. But my dark magic will give you a lot more juice. And you might need it to go so far back in time."

Jess narrows her eyes at me. She's made it clear that she doesn't want me using my dark magic, and I can't imagine the idea of me pushing it to her through our coven link is something she's keen on either. "Just normal blood, thanks," she says.

I let out a breath. "Look, I get it. I'm off my game and it's the dark magic's fault. It's likely to push me towards making bad decisions like filing my teeth into points and not bathing as often as I should. But right now? We need it. I don't think you'll be able to get far enough back in time without it."

Jess swallows hard. The fear from last night is visible in her eyes again. "Maybe this is a bad idea—"

"It's the only idea we have," I snap. "Jeqabeel is getting stronger. We have no other ideas. We *need* you to go back in time, Jess. And my dark magic is the only way you'll get there."

"I volunteer my blood for your dark magic." Xander pushes up his sleeve, displaying one large bicep threaded with corded muscle. "You should try not to use the dark magic, Saff, but this is an exception. We want Jess to get there safely."

Jess nods slowly. "I guess you're right. Use it this once and then lay off it, okay?"

"I already said I would." I take the knife Jess offers me, trying not to look too eagerly at Xander's muscled bicep.

As much as I hate to hurt him, I'm already craving the intoxicating rush of dark magic his blood will give me.

It's all I can do not to lick my lips, but I do my best to act reluctant. "You ready?" I ask him, hovering the knife over his arm.

He nods, pushing his sleeve up further. "I might not have magical powers, but this is something I can do."

"What about you?" I ask Jess. "Are you ready?"

"I'm not sure." She presses the blade to her hand. "How much of my own blood do you think I'll need?"

"A big cut," I tell her. "Enough to power a major spell. But not so much that you bleed out."

"Okay." She drags in a breath. "Then I guess I'm ready."

I hesitate for a moment with the knife on Xander's unmarked skin, savoring the excitement that thrums through me. The *anticipation*. I can only hope my eyes aren't sparkling, and that he thinks my hand is trembling because I'm reluctant to cut him.

"Do it, Saffy." Xander gives me a nod.

I bring the knife down on his arm, slicing a deep cut into his flesh.

My dark power fills me. The rush is overwhelming, and it's all I can do not to gasp with pleasure. For a long moment, I refuse to part with it because I'm too busy revelling in the way it makes me feel. Then I force myself to push it to Jess through our coven connection.

Jess's eyes widen as she feels it pour into her, and the color rushes into her cheeks. Her eyes darken, her irises turning black. A small smile tugs her lips up.

"Holy crap," she murmurs. "That's intense." She brings her knife down on her palm, slicing it wide open so her blood spills freely.

Then she vanishes.

I sag, my body drained. I stare at the empty space for several long seconds while my brain tries to catch up with what just happened. Every cell in my body feels empty and sad. Not because Jess is gone, but because my glorious power has been drained.

"I don't think I'll ever get used to that," says Xander. He walks into the kitchen and grabs a dishcloth to wrap the wound on his arm.

"Me neither." I force myself to stay where I am and not stop him from covering it up. A voice in my head is whispering that I could draw more power from that blood to replace what I lost. And if I just cut him a little deeper, inflicted a little more pain, I could...

I shake my head, and head to the bathroom to find a proper bandage for him. I could try to heal his cut, but the temptation to take more of his blood is so strong, I don't trust myself to get that close to the wound. I don't even think I can dress it for him. Instead I stand in the doorway, and throw him the bandage before turning away, clenching my hands into fists.

I'm both exhausted and bereft. And I hate that instead of worrying about Jess, I have to keep swallowing down a hard knot of regret and quietening the voice that keeps repeating how foolish I was for giving away all my power to her.

"My wound is covered," says Xander. "You can come back now." Surprised, I turn to him. I thought I'd been doing a reasonable job of hiding my blood lust, but I guess I was wrong.

"Were we crazy to push Jess into doing this?" I drag my mind away from my own disturbing needs. "Did we do the right thing?"

"We did the only thing we could." Xander puts an arm around my shoulders and I force myself to lean into his warmth, and think only about that and not about the dark magic or my worry for Jess.

We've already lost Rebecca. I can't bear to think of Jess running out of power and getting stuck in the Nowhere. It would be her worst nightmare. The worst possible way to die.

Shouldn't she be back by now? I thought her return would be almost instantaneous for us, but she's been gone several minutes.

What if she doesn't come back at all?

Chapter Nineteen

"How long do you think it'll be until Jess…?"

The hair stands up all over my body as Xander's voice trails off. My skin tingles.

And then Jess is here.

With a wompf of displaced air, she's standing in the center of the living room.

No, there are two people here. Two women, with their hands linked together.

Jess looks terrible. Her face is gray and drawn. Her eyes are bloodshot and she's shaking. A trickle of blood oozes from her nose.

The woman she's with lets go of Jess's hands. She's wearing a floating flowery dress, and her hair is long and blonde, just like Jess's.

"Are you alright, love?" asks the strange woman. Her voice is hoarse and croaky. "Drink some water," she adds. "Sit down and hydrate."

"I'll get water. " Xander starts toward the kitchen.

"Who are you?" I ask, although I'm pretty certain I

know. She looks like Jess, though she's not that much older than her. She's probably only about thirty.

"I'm Cybil." The woman puts her arm around Jess, steering her to one of the couches. "Sit down, sweetheart."

"This is my Mom," croaks Jess, her voice like rocks over concrete. She sits heavily, looking like she's going to faint.

"You did it." My knees feel weak with relief, and I collapse onto the other couch.

"She did." Cybil rubs one hand along Jess's arm. "She's incredibly strong. I knew she would be."

Jess sags against the arm of the couch, half lying down with her eyes shut.

"Is she going to be okay?" I ask Cybil.

"It was a big jump, going so far back. She's exhausted." Cybil doesn't seem to be showing the same signs of magic depletion. She looks tired, sure, but nothing like Jess.

Xander comes back in with two glasses of water and an unopened packet of marshmallows. "For sugar," he explains.

Jess gulps down some water. Her mother takes smaller sips, watching Jess with a worried gaze.

"That's better," sighs Jess. "I'm okay." She takes a marshmallow and puts it in her mouth, sighing with appreciation. "Where'd you find these?"

Xander shrugs. "One of the high cupboards."

Jess is still shaking, and keeps looking at her mother, almost like she's checking to make sure she's still there. "Mom came with me," she says, like she still can't believe it. "I wasn't strong enough to stay in the past. The present was pulling me back here."

Her mother nods. "Jess isn't as practised at resisting the pull as I am. We wouldn't have been able to talk for long if she'd tried to stay."

"You can resist the pull back to the present?" I ask.

"For a while. Maybe twenty-four hours, if I'm lucky." She smiles. "I know some techniques."

"I'm sorry, I haven't introduced myself. I'm Saffy, and this is Xander." I stick out my hand.

"Jess told me about you. " She takes my hand, while I try not to freak out about the fact that I'm shaking the hand of someone who's from eighteen years in the past.

Xander offers his hand. "Did Jess tell you what's happening?" he asks.

"About the demon? Yes, she did. That's why I came forward."

"We were told one of the rules was not to go forward in time," says Xander.

"It's not usually advisable," she agrees. "But Jess and I were able to jump together, and it's worth the risk to help her." Her eyes are misty, and she rubs Jess's arm again. It must have been weird for her to meet her adult daughter.

Even weirder for Jess, who hasn't seen her mother since she was six. The way she's looking at her now makes my throat close and tears prickle behind my eyes. The naked longing in her face... that's how I'd look if I had the chance to see my mother again.

"Mom, you need to eat and rest. You must be tired."

"No darling, I'm fine. Here, you lie down on the couch. You're the one who needs to rest." She smiles. "You did well, my love. I'm so proud of you."

Jess does what she says, stretching out on the couch and closing her eyes. She gives a deep sigh, and I'm pretty sure she's going to fall asleep.

I put my hand on Cybil's arm to draw her a little distance away, and keep my voice low so I don't wake Jess. "If you can only stay for a short time, we should talk about the demon. Jess needs to know how to use her power.

We're planning for her to go back in time and stop it from getting free."

Her mother raises her eyebrows. "How do you intend to stop it?"

"It was imprisoned in a bone. All Jess needs to do is make sure Jeqabeel can't get out of that bone." Xander keeps his voice as low as ours.

"Hmm." Cybil looks doubtful. "That may be easier said than done. What else do you know about the demon?"

"We know that my ancestors were the ones who imprisoned it in the bone. They put it in there in the eighteen hundreds, and Jeqabeel was safely trapped until my uncle came under the demon's spell."

Helpfully, the opening pages of Arabella's book rise up onto my skin, red letters clearly visible. "We have this book, which says..."

"How are you doing that?" interrupts Cybil. Her eyes go wide as she stares at the cursive letters which have appeared on my skin.

Her shock confirms my suspicion that witches didn't absorb spells in her time, just as I don't know anyone else who can do it in my time. But I have no idea why the idea's never caught on. Being able to drag spells inside me has made my magic stronger and easier to use, and made me a lot more powerful.

"The book had a spell in it called *Binde Magick*," I tell her. "It lets me absorb magic straight from the pages of a grimoire."

"I've never heard of anyone being able to do that."

"Anyway," I draw her back to what's important. "What do you think the dedication means? It was addressed to me, or someone with my name. I can't help but wonder if it's trying to tell me something."

She peers at the words, reading them under her breath.

"Time jumpers often compare time to yarn or string," she muses. "It says to go to the start of the strands, but it's vague. If it is meant for you, maybe it's agreeing with your current plan to secure the bone. Or perhaps it's telling you to find the person who first brought the demon to this dimension. Demons can't come here of their own free will. They must be called."

"How do we find out when the demon was called here?" I ask. "We have no idea when Jeqabeel arrived. And if we find that person, what would we do to them? Kill them?"

Xander shakes his head. "We're not even certain that the dedication has anything to do with what we're facing."

Cybil cocks her head as though listening to something. Then she frowns, turning toward the bookcase. "What's that?" She points at the pentagramic antiprism.

"We found it downstairs, in a safe." Xander picks it up and hands it to her. "We're not sure what it is, but the Unseen must have thought it was important, because he had it hidden."

"It must be from one of the demon dimensions." Cybil examines it gingerly, like it might bite her.

"How do you know?" I ask.

"Time magic has a frequency. A certain energy, if you like. I can feel a discordant energy coming from this bone that sets my teeth on edge, and I recognize the feeling."

"The energy's like yours?" I ask, trying to understand.

"Not like mine, but not unlike it, either." She shakes her head. "It's difficult to explain, but our magic allows us to travel through time and space, and pass alongside other dimensions. This feels like it's from one of those dimensions. Of all the magics, ours is most attuned to the demon realms."

Jess makes a sound, and when I turn, she's sitting up on

the couch, staring at her mother with a shocked expression. "We're related to demons?" she demands.

"Of course not, my love." Cybil gives a small laugh, sitting next to Jess on the couch. "Though some say that our magic originated from a witch who passed through a demon barrier. And demons can live in the folds between times, as well as other dimensions, so we sometimes pass their magic when we time jump. I simply recognise the feel of the magic."

Jess shudders. "So that thing's demonic?"

"I think so."

I sink into the chair opposite them. "Could it have been carved from a demon's bone?" I glance at Xander as he sits on the arm of my chair. The pentagram could have come from the creature in the drawing. Why else would the Unseen have it there?

She nods. "It certainly feels that way. It's a pentagram, a shape with power. They used pentagrams in ancient times for trapping demonic essences."

My mouth drops open and I gape at her, every synapse in my brain lighting up at once. "You can imprison a demon inside this thing?" I meet Xander's gaze, my heart speeding up. He looks just as excited as I feel.

"This could be just what we need to control the demon," he says. "The Unseen might have been evil incarnate, but he was a smart guy. He was keeping it as an insurance policy against Jeqabeel."

Cybil smiles at us both, her eyes shining. "You're right. This could be exactly what is needed. Legend says this shape helps to render a demon powerless."

"And if it's made from demon bone, Jeqabeel won't be able to consume it." I smile back at her. "This is perfect."

"You really think we can trap the demon inside it?" Jess asks. "How would we do that?"

"Except…" Xander looks doubtful.

"What?" I demand.

"Well, why hasn't anyone else tried using a pentagram, if it's so perfect?" he asks.

"Good question," I say slowly. "Surely the others in the council would have suggested trying something like this?"

Cybil shakes her head. "I don't know how you got hold of a pentagram carved from demon bone, but I've never heard of the existence of anything like this before. This artefact is one of a kind. Besides, it's only thanks to my magic that I recognize the object's potential."

But now that I've started thinking it through, other problems are poking into the plan. "Jeqabeel's not an ordinary demon any more," I say to Cybil. "It's got Dallas's power, plus the council's. It's really strong."

Cybil sighs. "Then its essence may be too difficult for even a powerful artefact like this to contain."

My heart sinks. "There must be a way we can try it. Maybe we could test it on Jeqabeel somehow?"

"You want to test it?" Jess sounds incredulous. "What do you suggest? We ask Jeqabeel if it'll pop into the nice little pentagramic antiprism so we can see if it'll hold it?"

Xander frowns. "What if we don't have to face the demon now? What if someone faced it back in time? *Before* Jeqabeel became so powerful?"

I blink at him.

"If the people who put the demon's essence into the bone had used something like the pentagram, it might not have gotten free." Xander looks at Cybil. "Is it possible you could go back in time and give this to the witches who put the demon into the bone? Tell them to use it instead?"

"When exactly did they do that?" asks Cybil.

Xander hesitates, then lets out a disappointed breath. "No idea."

"I know." My voice rises with fresh excitement. "Remember that drawing that Dallas's wife Mireya showed us before she was killed? She had a picture of the demon destroying the Library of Congress. It had killed a lot of people, and the witches of the time blamed the deaths on a hurricane to cover up what really happened. That's when they trapped it in the bone."

He snaps his fingers. "That's right. It was in the late eighteen hundreds. Eighteen ninety… something. Do you remember the year?"

I shake my head.

Cybil raises her eyebrows. "Go back in time to the eighteen hundreds?" She glances at Jess and then me. "It'd be a very dangerous jump."

"But it's possible?"

Again, she looks between Jess and me. Her gaze is so intense, it makes me want to fidget under her scrutiny. I hold my breath while we wait for her answer.

"I think so." She sighs, not sounding happy about it.

My heart lifts again, my excitement rising another notch. "Then it *is* the perfect solution. The demon was far weaker then. We know those witches managed to imprison it in the bone, so we just give them the pentagram thingy and they can use that instead. Easy."

"Not if Mom dies trying to get there," Jess objects. "She said it would be dangerous." She shifts to sit closer to her mother. "I've been without you for years. I don't want to lose you again."

Cybil wraps an arm around Jess. "Sweetheart, you don't understand. The only place I can go from here is back to my own time. Besides, I'm not strong enough to jump back that far."

"What?" Jess jerks her face back. "You want *me* to go all that way back in time?"

"I don't *want* you to do it. All I'm saying is that I think you could."

"But how?" Jess shakes her head. "I don't know anything about my magic. Everything I've done so far has been guesswork."

"Sweetheart, you just jumped back almost twenty years without any training at all. Do you have any idea how impressive that is?" Cybil's eyes shine. "Imagine what you'll be able to do with a little help."

"So you'll jump back in time with me?" Jess asks.

Cybil shakes her head, her eyes crinkled with regret. "I wish I could, my darling, but like I said, the only place I can go from here is back home to my present day."

Jess's face crumples. "There's no way we could do it together?"

"I'm sorry." She puts both arms around Jess, hugging her close, and it seems like a private moment, so I pretend I need something from the kitchen to give them some space.

Xander follows me into the kitchen. Ratticus is lying on his back inside a bowl that must have once been full of food. He's fast asleep, making small snuffly noises that sound remarkably like snores.

"What do you think"? I ask Xander quietly. "Is it too dangerous to send Jess back so far in time?"

"If her mother thinks she can do it, then she probably can."

I nod, but still feel uneasy about asking her to do something so risky. Especially because I've time travelled with Jess and felt for myself how scary it is. Getting caught in the Nowhere would be worse than being a statue, or anything else I could imagine.

"The first step is finding out exactly when and where she'd need to jump back to." Xander sounds thoughtful.

"We need to find the exact date of the hurricane. It must have been recorded."

My lips twitch. "Is Detective Trent on the case? "

He grimaces. "Speaking of which, my boss has been calling. Apparently I won't be a detective for much longer if I don't turn up to work." He shrugs. "Not that it matters if the city burns."

"As soon as we've saved the world, you can be a detective again."

"Jess's phone died, didn't it?" he asks. "Mine's out of charge too. And the Unseen doesn't seem to have a computer or a television set, let alone a phone charger." He looks around for the car keys, and picks them up. "I'll have to do this the old fashioned way. I'll go and look for a library or Internet cafe, so I can look up the date of the hurricane."

"I'll go with you," I say, not wanting him to head out alone.

But he shakes his head. "You should stay here and learn more about time travel from Cybil. I assume Jess will need your power to go back that far in time."

Oh crap. He's right.

"Yeah, I'll probably need to go with her to give Jess enough power," I say casually, pretending I'd figured that out already. "We'll have to go back to the eighteen hundreds together."

Chapter Twenty

After Xander leaves, I head back into the living room, where Jess and her mother are sitting on the couch, deep in a serious discussion.

"Why did you disappear when I was six?" Jess is asking. "What happened?"

"Isn't it obvious?" Cybil asks gently. "I disappeared because I came here. You brought me to this time."

Maybe their conversation is supposed to be private, but I have too many questions not to interrupt. "How can it have happened already when we hadn't done it yet?" I perch on the arm of the couch.

"It's hard to explain," says Cybil. "The way we think about time isn't strictly correct, because time isn't linear. Think of it as a loose ball of yarn with strands that intersect."

I still don't get it. Trying to figure out time travel is like wondering whether the chicken or the egg came first. Nothing about it makes any sense.

Jess is looking worried. "Have I messed up the timeline by bringing you here? When I was a kid, you never came home again. So if you leave here now, does that mean you won't make it back to your own time?"

I swallow. I hadn't considered the question of why Cybil never made it home. Is Jeqabeel destined to kill us all and that's why she can't jump back to her own time?

No, I don't believe that. I can't believe it.

Cybil nods, her eyes sad. "There must be a reason I don't go back. It's possible I severed the link to my present day. There's a spell that will cut the strand that's pulling me back, so I can stay here."

Jess brightens. "You'll stay here with me?"

Cybil smiles sadly. "I can if I cut myself off from my magic completely. But it'll mean I won't be able to help you any more. I'll be a mundane." She keeps her tone level, like it's no big deal, but I catch a hint of reluctance in her expression before she can hide it.

Jess must catch it too, because she shakes her head. "No, you can't do that. Why don't you tell me what we need to know, then go back to your own time. Can't you change things so you can be with me and Dad back then?"

"No, my darling. For some reason that didn't happen, and trying to change it could create consequences we can't imagine." Her tone is gentle. "If I disappeared, I must have come here and severed the link." She shoots me a glance as though silently telling me not to argue. "I must have chosen to stay in your time. It's the only explanation."

Even though time travel makes my brain hurt, I can't argue with her logic. Especially if the alternative is that we all die.

"I don't understand anything about the magic." Jess scrubs her palms over her eyes. "Tell me how it works."

"Okay. But you should eat something first." Her worried eyes rove over Jess's face, as though checking for signs that her daughter needs fattening up. "You need to keep your strength up, sweetheart."

"I'll heat up the leftover stew." I stand and head to the kitchen.

Ratticus makes a half-snore, half-snorting noise, as though he's just woken up. *"I could eat more stew,"* he mumbles.

I turn at the door. "Would you like some stew, Cybil? Or a hot drink? There's instant coffee, but no cream."

Cybil gives me a smile. "Black coffee sounds perfect. Thank you."

After heating up stew for Jess and making coffee for her mother, I give Ratticus some more food. "Do you ever stop eating?" I ask, ladling stew into his plate.

"Not unless I have to," he says with his mouth full.

When I go back into the living room, carrying the stew and coffee, Cybil is explaining how time jumping works.

"You can't go to the future. Only back to the past." She winks. "But you can still call me *Doc*."

I groan at her terrible joke. The only reason I have any idea what she's talking about is thanks to my father's eighties-only TV. I've watched the first two *Back To The Future* movies more than once.

Cybil's grin lightens her face, showing how beautiful she actually is. How did Magnus manage to score a wife like her when he's such a grumpy old coot?

But maybe Magnus is only grumpy because his wife vanished when their daughter was young, and he never saw her again. If so, I'm partially to blame for helping send Jess to the past to fetch her.

"You came forward in time," Jess points out, tapping the leather arm of the couch.

"Only with your guidance. To time jump, you need to have a clear picture of where you're going. That's not usually possible if you're jumping into the future, at least not with one hundred percent certainty. Going into the past, you can use a strong memory of a place you know well, and be confident it will be there just as you remember, with no nasty surprises."

"We're not going to have memories of the eighteen hundreds."

Jess is right, it's a big hole in our plan.

"You can use photographs," says Cybil. "Memories work best, but it's possible to go back in time to a place you never were."

"Possible? Like theoretically?" Jess is still tapping the arm of the couch, except now it's a tune. I think I recognise Seven Nation Army by the White Stripes.

"I've never done it myself." Cybil hesitates, her brow furrowed. "Maybe I shouldn't have suggested it. I don't know whether I'm more afraid of encouraging you to jump so far back, or what the demon will do if you can't stop it." She leans over to squeeze Jess's arm. "But even as as a baby you were incredibly strong. You started time jumping when you were five years old, and we'd never heard of anyone being able to jump that young. The first time you did it, you came back dirty and crying. We were so worried about you. Your father was terrified."

"That's when you bound my magic?"

"No, I would never…" She shakes her head. "Your father must have done that after I disappeared. Maybe he was worried that whatever had happened to me might also happen to you."

"He lied to me and told me I had no magic. He made me feel like an outcast." Jess's lip curls. "I've lived my entire life with the feeling there was something missing. Even now, knowing what my magic is, I'm scared to use it. If he'd been honest with me, everything might have been different. But my own father was too much of a coward to tell me the truth."

"He must have had a good reason. He was so afraid of losing you."

"Maybe because I made him look bad in front of the Blood Council?" Jess mutters, her expression dark.

"I'm sure that's not the reason..."

Jess makes an impatient movement with her hand. "How do you think he got to be head of the council?"

"Whatever his reasoning, it doesn't matter right now," I interrupt. "I'm sorry, Jess, I really am. But we don't have time for this. We have to figure out how to get back to the eighteen hundreds."

Jess leans back and nods. "You're right. Keep going, Mom. Tell me more about how the magic works."

Cybil hesitates as if she'd like to say more on the subject, then sighs.

"If you're going to use an image rather than a memory, make sure you know exactly *when* you're going, and what the place looks like. You don't want to land in the middle of a concrete wall."

I wince. "That sounds unpleasant."

"There's a reason there aren't very many of us," says Cybil.

"Bad sense of direction?" I joke.

She frowns at my glibness. "The most important thing to remember is not to change the past. Remember how I said time was like a ball of yarn? Well every minute is made up of millions of events, all inter-connected, like fibers that make up the strand. If you break one fiber by changing something that's already happened, it weakens the yarn. Break enough of them, and the whole thing could start to unravel."

Jess blinks, her expression alarmed. "Time can unravel? Has that ever happened?"

"Not for many generations. Generally, once time has been spun, and all the fibers are in place, they resist change. For example, my beloved dog, my childhood pet, was killed in a car accident when I was eleven. I decided to go back and save Trixie, in spite of my mother forbidding it."

"Did you save Trixie?" I ask.

She shakes her head. "I saved her from the car accident, but not from death. I went back to the morning she was due to escape from our yard onto the road, and made sure she was securely shut in."

"So how did she die?" asks Jess.

"She dropped dead anyway. Died in our front yard at exactly the same time as the car was supposed to have hit her." Cybil looks sad. "The vet said she must have had an undiagnosed heart condition, but I know she died because the strands of time had already been woven into place. It's probably a good thing I wasn't able to break them. Who knows what might have happened?"

"You said if you break enough strands, time itself could start to unravel?" I ask.

"That's right. I was taught that many centuries ago, a reckless witch caused an entire continent to be erased from the map. All memory of the place was wiped out as though it never existed." She raises her eyebrows at us. "Mundanes still talk about Atlantis as though it's a mythical island that somehow sunk beneath the waves. But Atlantis simply vanished from the Earth when its thread unravelled. No trace will ever be found, because its timeline was unwritten."

Jess and I exchange an incredulous look. "So if I mess up, I could unwrite an entire timeline?" she demands. "Why does anyone ever risk going back in time?"

"That's why I'm here." Her mother takes her hand. "I'll help you avoid those kinds of mistakes. You need to be careful to change as little as possible."

"But I'm about to try to change *everything*." Jess pulls her hand away, her face reddening. "We're attempting to stop Jeqabeel from ever escaping. If we're successful, Saffy's parents won't die, and neither will her uncle, or cousin, or a whole bunch of other people."

"What you're doing is risky, sweetheart, there's no doubt about that. And if you're successful, those people may die anyway, just like Trixie did." She looks over at me apologetically. "The strands of the past have already been woven, and they'll try to remain that way."

"But we could also cause the whole timeline to unravel? Make millions of people disappear under the sea?" I ask, ready to call the whole plan off.

"The alternative isn't terribly appealing either," Cybil points out. "If you do nothing, the demon will raze Baltimore, and probably the rest of the world, to the ground."

"This is a nightmare." Jess is drumming on the couch again, her fingers tapping out a complicated beat. "If I mess up, I destroy the world. But if I don't try, the world gets destroyed anyway."

"Sweetie, we'll talk through it before you go, and make sure—"

"But you won't be coming with me," Jess interrupts. "I'll be on my own, using a power I know nothing about."

"I'll be with you," I say quietly.

"But you're not the one who'll be responsible if it all goes wrong." Jess stands up, shaking her head. "I can't deal with this. I never asked for it. A few days ago, I had no magic at all, and now I could destroy the whole world?"

She storms to the door. "No way. I'm not doing it. Let somebody else deal with it, because I can't."

She disappears down the hallway. Cybil and I stare at each other. Given that Jess is usually the calmest person in a crisis, I'm not sure how to deal with this reaction. And Cybil looks as dismayed and uncertain as I am.

"I'm handling this all wrong." Cybil rubs her forehead. "I'm used to having a six-year-old daughter, not a woman in her twenties. It's a little disorientating for me, too."

"She's just upset. She'll come round." I stand up. "Let me talk to her."

I discover Jess sitting on the floor in the bedroom, leaning against the wall. She's got her knees folded up in front of her, and her arms wrapped around her legs.

"We need you," I say simply. "The demon won't stop until everyone is dead."

"I know." she sighs. "I've always wished I was magical, and now I have this stupid power that could do more harm than good. If I screw up, I could turn America into Atlantas. It's a lot, you know?"

I sit next to her, my shoulder touching hers. "I know. All our choices are bad ones, and we're running out of time. I don't want to use my dark magic either. But that's what I have to do. It's the only way." I nudge her shoulder. "At least if we screw up, we'll be doing it together."

She drops her head onto her knees. "This sucks."

"I know it does. But we're strong enough to survive it."

"You sure about that?"

"We survived that mosh pit in Philly didn't we? And getting unfairly arrested that time in Dallas, when we'd done nothing wrong?" I nudge her again. "You want to know what I think? Compared to being in front of the stage at a Butthole concert, what we're planning will be a walk in the park."

Jess lifts her face and grimaces. "Fine. Let's do it. Let's destroy the world."

"That's the spirit." I jump to my feet and offer her my hand to help her up.

When we go back to the living room, Cybil's pacing back and forth between the couches. She gives us a relieved look.

"Sorry about that." Jess sits on the couch. "I know we have a lot to get through, and limited time. So keep talking. Tell me more about time jumping."

Cybil sits beside her. "The most important thing I need to tell you is about the Nowhere." She shudders. "The last thing you want is to ever end up there."

"Been there, done that," says Jess. "Got the Nowhere T-shirt."

"You've been to the Nowhere?" Her mother looks horrified. "But you're okay?" She runs her gaze over Jess as though she can't believe she doesn't have any visible wounds.

"You haven't been there?" Jess asks.

"Of course not. It's the first lesson I learned. The Nowhere is terribly dangerous. It'll suck the magic out of you, and if you're too weak when you arrive, you may never escape it."

Jess and I exchange a glance.

"I'm so sorry," her mother is clearly distressed. "Landing there must have been terrifying."

Jess nods. "Tell you the truth, I'd really like to never go there again."

Cybil lets out a huff of breath. "My mother warned me that if I accidentally landed in the Nowhere, I'd be dead in a few minutes. So for the first few years of my training, I only did very short jumps to places I knew well."

"The first few *years*?" I can't hold back my shock.

Jess scrunches her face. "We don't have time for that kind of training. When I went back eighteen years to get you, I managed to avoid the Nowhere. How does that rate?"

"Even with all my training, I've never tried jumping that far back. I don't think I have that much power."

Jess blinks. "Really? You haven't jumped back eighteen years, but you think we can go back to the eighteen hundreds?"

I can't imagine how this must be messing with Jess's head. I reach out and grab her hand. What if she hadn't been powerful enough? She might have ended up stuck in the Nowhere, the one place that scares the living crap out of her.

"That type of jump would be too difficult for *most* time jumpers," Cybil says. "But in our family line, there have always been those who were more powerful. I've seen photos..." she trails off, as if stuck in the memory.

"Photos?"

"Of three women, who look identical, but for their ages. The same person, at three different stages of their life." She smiles at Jess. "You're already far stronger than I am, and with the help of Saffy's dark magic, I think you can do anything."

As if summoned by the mention, my dark magic rises and I'm hit by a wave of desire for Jess's blood. When I used it to kill the Unseen, it was like nectar from the gods. If we're to go back in time, whose blood will I use? Will I get to draw in Jess's magic again? All I can think about is the intoxicating rush of power it gave me.

"Saffy, are you okay?"

It takes a moment or two for the question to break into my thoughts. When I manage to focus on them, both Jess and Cybil are frowning at me. I shake my head, trying to

rid myself of the memory. "I'm fine." I motion to Jess. "Anyway, what were you saying?"

"What are you—?" Jess breaks off as we hear the sound of a car screeching to a rapid stop outside.

Jumping up, I reach the window in time to see Xander leap out of the car and race up the driveway toward the front door.

My heart clenches. Something has to be terribly wrong.

Chapter Twenty-One

I rush to the door and fling it open. As soon as I step outside, I can smell smoke.

Xander looks shocked. His face is pale and his expression tight. He drags me inside and slams the door shut behind us.

"What's the matter?" I demand. "Are you okay?"

"Baltimore is burning. Rebecca's vision is coming true."

My face drains of blood and behind me, Jess curses.

"What's burning?" I step back, giving Xander room to speak to all three of us.

"Everything. Houses. Offices. Cars. I barely made it out of the library before it went up in flames." He drags a shaking hand through his hair. "People are trapped in buildings or running through the streets. Hundreds are dying. Maybe thousands."

My heart feels as heavy as rock, so heavy that every beat hurts. "We have to do something. We need to help them."

Ratticus must have been roused by the commotion,

because he pokes his head into the hallway, his whiskers twitching. "*Help them?*" he repeats incredulously. "*They're doomed. We need to find somewhere to hide.*"

"That's not all." Xander sounds grim. "I saw the demon. It's not trying to hide anymore. It's openly killing people, and being broadcast on every TV station."

Ratticus squeaks and scuttles into the living room, presumably looking for somewhere to hole up.

"Shit." I swallow, seeing the shock I'm feeling reflected on the faces of Jess and her mother. It feels like our world just shifted on its axis. After centuries of staying hidden, everyone now knows about witches and demons.

"Apparently, the President sent in a team of army rangers," Xander follows Ratticus into the living room. "The rangers were supposed to take out the demon."

"What happened?" asks Jess.

"Jeqabeel ripped their heads off on live television."

"Ohmygod." I put my hand over my mouth. Jess and I share a horrified look. Cybil sinks onto one of the couches, her face pale.

"What about your mother?" I ask. "Is she still in the demon's thrall?"

Xander's mouth draws down. "I don't know. She wasn't in any of the news reports I saw. I'm...afraid she might be dead."

"I'm so sorry, Xander." I put my hand on his arm, wishing I could do more.

"I should have tried to call her, at least. Maybe I could have gotten her away from the demon."

"Your phone died," I point out. "Anyway, you didn't know she'd be in so much danger."

"Yeah, but I should have." He sounds furious with himself.

"We've barely had time to catch our breaths," I say.

"We've hardly slept and we're all still exhausted and on edge. There's nothing we could have done for your mother."

Any more than we could have saved Rebecca. My stomach clenches at the thought of the young girl in Jeqabeel's hands.

"We can fix this." Jess lifts her chin. "We have to."

I nod firmly, trying to put my fear for Rebecca out of my head. "Did you find anything useful while you were out?"

Xander tugs a piece of paper out of his other pocket. "I have the information on where you need to go." He hands me a picture that looks like it's been torn from a book. It's an old black and white photo of the Library of Congress. It's not fully built, it's got scaffolding all around it, and bricks in piles.

"There was a hurricane in eighteen ninety four, while it was being built. Lots of people died. They blamed it on the unsafe structure, and the impact of the storm." He points to a date scrawled underneath the photo. "That's the day the storm hit, when all the people were killed."

The year is familiar, and I scratch around in my memory. Why does eighteen ninety four ring a bell? Have I read something about it recently?

Cybil peers over my shoulder at the photo. "The picture is good enough," she says. "And there's a clear spot there, on the stairs." She looks at Jess. "You think you'll be able to hold this image clearly in your mind? You'll need to memorize it exactly, and manifest it to appear around you."

I'm only half listening, because the eighteen ninety four thing is bugging me. I reach inside myself, searching for the reference I half remember, and words rise to the surface of my skin. It's the publishing information at the back of Arabella Lightfoot's book.

Published by Arabella Lightfoot
East Capitol Street, Washington DC
December 9, 1894

It's the same date Xander scribbled at the bottom of the photograph. The same day as the storm. It's too much of a coincidence not to be relevant.

"Look at this." I thrust out my arm to show the others.

"The Thomas Jefferson building is on East Capitol Street in Washington," says Jess. "Is that the original Library of Congress building?"

"I think so," says Xander. "According to what I read, there are four buildings now, but it's the original one that was destroyed by the demon."

Cybil frowns at the words on my arm. "The book must have been written to give you this information. It's confirming the time and place of where you need to go "

"You can go back to an exact date?" I ask Jess.

She nods. "I think so."

"What about going from Baltimore to Washington? Does distance matter?" I look at Cybil.

"Washington is close enough that you should be able to get there in one jump," she replies.

"It's going back a hundred and twenty five years that has me worried," says Jess.

Her mother gives her a reassuring smile. "With Saffy providing the power, you can do it. I know you can."

It feels good to finally have a concrete plan, and I let out a long breath. "What else do we need to know before we give it a try?"

"I need to practise jumping back in time," says Jess. "And Mom needs to tell me a lot more about how—"

A roaring noise interrupts her, and she looks around

with a puzzled expression. It's like nothing I've heard before, a sound that seems to be coming from all around rather than a single direction. And it's getting louder.

The broken window in the living room is in a sheltered spot, so up until now I haven't felt more than a light breeze come in through it. But the wind is building. It's whistling in, lifting our hair and rustling the drawings pinned to the walls.

"What's going on?" Xander rushes to the broken window to peer through it, then tries to see out one of the windows on the street side of the house. By his puzzled expression, I can tell he can't see anything.

"It's Dallas." My heart starts thudding. "It has to be. He's coming for us."

"You need to do the time jump now," says Cybil. "You can't wait any longer."

"But I don't know enough." Jess looks dismayed. "I have no idea what I'm doing."

Cybil puts her hand on Jess's arm, her eyes full of love. "I wouldn't let you do it if I didn't think you could, sweetheart. And I'm going to sever my connection to the magic so my own time won't pull me away. I'll be here when you get back."

"But—"

"I believe in you." The wind's getting so loud, Cybil has to shout over the roar. "You know everything you need to. I promise."

Jess nods, but she still looks afraid. "Okay. We'll go."

Xander grabs my arms, gazing into my eyes. "Are you sure, Saff? You think this is the right thing to do?"

I swallow, far from sure about anything. "This is the only thing we *can* do," I say honestly. Though we don't have time to waste, I rise up on tiptoe and press my lips to his. I wish I didn't have to leave him. Especially now Dallas has arrived.

"I'll put wards in place around the house." I yell the words so they can all hear me. "I won't leave you undefended."

Cybil shakes her head. "We won't need them. As far as Xander and I are concerned, you'll be back a few seconds after you leave."

"Still." There's no way I'm leaving them vulnerable. The wind's gusting so strongly that the glass in the windows is flexing, and they could blow in at any moment.

"Saffy." Xander takes my hands. "Don't waste your power. You'll need it all to get where you're going. The important thing is containing the demon."

"But—" I hesitate, then nod. Mostly because I don't want to say what I'm thinking out loud. The truth is, if we don't make it back, that means we'll have failed. And if we can't find a way to stop the demon, the entire city will be undefended, not just Xander.

Xander pulls up his sleeve. "Have you got a knife? Take my blood. As much as you need."

I hesitate. My dark magic prefers pain and suffering. I mean, I've used Xander's blood like this before, offered up freely. But the dark magic spells I was casting were much smaller. They were part of my own magic. This time, I'm helping Jess, through our coven link, to go back in time further than any witch in recorded history has gone.

We're going to need much, much more of my dark magic.

Xander's blood freely given might not be enough to get Jess and me back to the eighteen hundreds.

I glance at Cybil. Her expression is troubled. She can see my dilemma, even if Xander can't.

Except how else am I going to get the blood I need?

There's no way I'd take any more from him by force. The blood Xander's offering will have to do.

I grab the knife from my pocket and bring it over Xander's arm, but before I can cut him, a fresh blast of wind hits me with such force that I stagger backward. With a deafening crash, the glass explodes out of all the windows. Xander reacts instantly, tackling me to the ground, covering me with his body. Shards of glass rain down around us.

I wouldn't have thought it could get any louder, but the roar filling my ears turns into a piercing shriek. Nails are tearing out of wood. Timber is snapping. Ceiling tiles are ripping free. The roof peels away like a can opening, until there's sky above us.

It's hard to keep my eyes open in the wind. It instantly whips all the moisture out of them, and makes my vision blur. But still, I see Dallas land just like Superman does in the movies, after he's been flying. Dallas drops gracefully onto his feet in what's left of the living room, near where we're huddling with our arms over our heads.

As soon as his feet touch the ground, the wind dies.

Dallas throws back his head and laughs. "Finally," he gloats. "I'm going to tear your head from your shoulders for what you did to Mireya."

Chapter Twenty-Two

Xander lets me go, and I struggle to my feet. We stand side by side, facing Dallas.

Dallas's white hair is sticking up in a halo around his head, and his expression is so gleeful it makes him look crazy. Hardly surprising, seeing as he was Jeqabeel's vessel until very recently. His pale eyes still glow a little red.

Weirdly, the main emotion I'm feeling right now is annoyance. I wish I could get it through Dallas's thick skull that I didn't kill Mireya. It feels like I'm about to be killed for a crime I didn't actually commit. Given all the things I've done recently that *are* against witch laws, it's…well, *annoying.*

Except, it doesn't really matter now. Dallas is clearly unhinged.

"You know the demon's just going to kill you, right?" I already know I'm wasting my breath. "When you're no use to it anymore?"

Dallas snarls and a gust of wind blasts my hair back, making me stagger. Overhead, the open sky has turned thunderous, dark grey clouds gathered in tall formations. Jess and Cybil are on the other side of the room, behind Dallas. Cybil is standing in front, holding Jess behind her, like she's going to protect her from Dallas's fury.

"Don't you dare speak to me," snarls Dallas. He lifts one hand and tendrils of his magic snake upward. The sky cracks overhead, the sound deafening. Lightning flashes down toward us, so bright it hurts my eyes.

"Take cover," Xander yells, tackling me to the floor, pushing me behind the couch.

Even with Xander shielding me with his body, the boom of thunder reverberates in my brain until I can't tell what's real and what's the echo. I feel like a drum being pounded by an angry heavy metal drummer. And the light is so bright, even with my eyes squeezed shut, it feels like it's burning my whole body.

Then the noise and light stop as though switched off. Xander's weight comes off me as he scrambles up to see what's happening. I pull myself up too, squinting through dazed eyes. What I see leaves me breathless.

Cybil must have rushed at Dallas. He's on the ground and she has her hands locked around his throat.

But attacking such a powerful witch that way is a crazy move that had to have been driven by pure desperation, and her momentary advantage doesn't last.

Dallas uses his magic to hurl Cybil away, tearing her hands loose. She slams against what's left of the far wall and lies still, as if she's been knocked unconscious. But Dallas scrambles back on his feet looking furious, and it's clear he hasn't finished with her. A powerful gust of wind picks up her body and throws her against the remains of the bookcase on the other side of the room. Debris and pieces of broken tile crash on top of her limp body from the gaping, broken roof above. Ratticus gives a terrified squeak, running out from where he must have been hiding amongst the fallen books and broken bookcase shelves.

"Mom!" Jess rushes to Cybil, dropping to her knees.

Dallas turns back to me, his eyes filled with a hot, dangerous rage.

"Is that the best you can do?" he snarls. He takes a step forward, then stops when a furry bundle runs over his foot.

Ratticus squeaks again, clearly disorientated as he searches for a new hiding place. He flicks his head back and forth as though deciding which way to run.

He's just the distraction I need.

My knife is still in my hand. Slicing my palm, I bring up runes from inside me to control my animal and earth magic. The runes write themselves into the skin on the undersides of my forearms. I can't access my dark magic, but my animal and earth might be strong enough to hold Dallas off. All I need to do is choose how best to use it.

Ratticus makes a break toward the door. With one swift movement Dallas bends and grabs him.

"Is this your pet?" he asks. "Watch me crush it." Dallas lifts Ratticus, tightening both hands around the rat's desperately struggling body.

Ratticus shrieks, a shrill sound of fear and pain. His voice fills my brain, so loud it sears through me, obliterating all thought. *Make him stop. MAKE HIM STOP!*"

I reel backward, clapping my hands over my ears, though there's no way to muffle Ratticus' screaming. It fills my head so I can't see or think about anything else.

The magic inside me reacts to my pain, surging out of my control. At the same time, the runes I'd brought up to control the magic vanish, wiped away in an instant by the clamor in my head.

My magic bursts free. It pours out of me, wild and

untamed and completely undirected, just like it used to before I had the spells to control it.

My earth magic slams into the ground at my feet. I'm thrown sideways as the ground erupts, rippling and rocking. I've created an earthquake, a surge of violent energy with no purpose and no thought, just a reaction to the intense pain of Ratticus's screams in my head.

My animal magic has always been even stronger and more chaotic. It bursts out of me with the force of a tsunami, flooding into Ratticus, the source of my pain.

The rat grows.

No, Ratticus doesn't just grow. He *explodes* outward. With a shout of surprise, Dallas drops him. Ratticus is doubling, tripling, quadrupling in size. Not just growing in size, his fur is becoming darker, matting together, spiking out like a giant porcupine. In the space of a blink, Ratticus is bigger than Dallas. Then I can't even see Dallas, because Ratticus's body blocks him from view. The rat is bigger than a car. Bigger than an elephant. He grows so fast, his body slams into me and pushes me backward, throwing me against the wall. His fur is dirty and rough, and I get a whiff of foul giant rat breath.

When Ratticus sits up on his haunches, his body takes up the entire living room. He's so big, his head projects way above where the roof used to be. His whiskers are like tree branches.

Ratticus's screams—the piercing shrieks that only I can hear—suddenly stop. The pain in my head vanishes. Now, I can think again. But the ground under my feet is still rolling and shaking, making me stagger wildly back and forth. I grab the wall for purchase, trying to stay on my feet.

Where is Dallas?

He must be behind Ratticus's enormous bulk, where I

can't see him. At any moment he could use his magic to blast apart Ratticus. And I can't do a thing to stop him because my own magic is now spent. I wasted it creating the biggest creature I've ever seen.

Cursing, I yank what's left of my earth magic back into myself, using a rune to control it again, and steadying the ground under my feet.

Then Ratticus shifts his weight, and when his immense foot crashes down, it shakes up the ground again, smashing up more of the floor. His squeaks are shrill, and his giant hairless tail flicks sideways. It slams into me, bowling me over.

"Stop, Ratticus!" I yell. "You're going to crush us all!"

Problem is I can't snatch the animal magic back from Ratticus like I did with my earth magic. The crazy, violent, *powerful* spell I cast has woven itself into Ratticus in a complicated tangle, with some of my earth magic snagged in. To unwind it, I need more magic. More blood.

I squeeze the wound I just cut into my hand, and more blood flows. But my magic is almost depleted, and feels pitifully weak without being able to use dark magic to supercharge it. I move around Ratticus, reaching for the strands of magic I can see covering him, determined to do what I can.

As I round his giant flank, Dallas comes into view. He's standing in front of Ratticus, staring up at him. His face is twisted with rage, his pale skin mottled red.

Dallas lifts his hand and black strands of oily magic extend out of him.

My chest clenches tight, fear filling me. If the demon is using Dallas as a conduit, Jeqabeel must be close. I can feel the demon's presence like a dark, heavy oil slick that's permeated the air around us.

"I'll tear you to pieces," roars Dallas, spittle flying from his lips. "I'll make you scream in agony and beg for mercy."

I'm not sure who he's talking to, but he's looking up at Ratticus like the giant rat is the cause of all his problems. I guess right now, he is.

The wind rises, strengthening so quickly that a gust knocks me back to the ground. The oily tentacles of Dallas's magic curl up toward Ratticus.

"Watch out, Ratticus," I shout, struggling to regain my feet against the gale swirling around me.

"My master is here!" Dallas yells over the roaring wind, his black magic oozing toward Ratticus. "My master will—"

"I need to hide!" squeals Ratticus, his voice hysterical in my head. His ears are twitching back and forth, and his eyes are wild. *"What have you done? I'm too big. There's nowhere to hide!"* He gives a loud screech, so high-pitched I cover my ears with my hands, trying to stop the pain. Ratticus twists his whole body blindly, and his tail flicks dangerously in my direction. Throwing myself back onto the ground, I narrowly miss being hit a second time.

But Dallas isn't so lucky. He takes the full force of Ratticus's hairless tail across his chest. The howling wind dies abruptly as Dallas is thrown backwards against the wall, next to where Jess is crouching over her mother. Dallas must be dazed, because he lifts his head slowly, turning to Jess. Then he lifts his hand as if to cast another spell.

Jess scrambles protectively in front of her mother's prone body. She picks up something on the floor next to her, and brings her arm down in a wide arc, hitting Dallas in the chest.

My dark magic surges as Dallas's powerful blood spurts from the wound. I can taste the blood in the back of my throat and my rush of longing for it is so strong it overwhelms me.

When Jess staggers backward I see her mother's ceremonial knife sticking out of Dallas's chest. His eyes are open, and he stares down at his chest in surprise.

As the blood drains from Dallas's face, I feel his life force leaving him. My dark magic is the only thing in control of my limbs as I stumble over to him. I feel his heart stutter and the last of the air in his lungs seep from his mouth. His magic is dying with him as I sink to my knees beside him, and all I can think about is soaking my hands in his blood and absorbing his powerful, irresistible magic before it can fade.

"Do something, stupid witch!" Ratticus screams in my head. *"More of them are coming. I can't hide!"* His shrill voice is like a slap across the face. It clears the haze of my dark bloodlust for a moment.

Jess cries out, her voice a desperate sob. "Help my mother, Saffy! She's not moving. You have to help her!"

As I look over at Jess and Cybil, Ratticus whirls around again and his tail slams into the wall next to us, bringing more debris raining down on us. The rat is desperately looking for an escape route, but the partially-destroyed walls are blocking his way, and he's too big to fit through any of the doors.

"You need to do something about Ratticus first." Xander drops to his knees beside me. "If you don't, he could crush us."

Swallowing hard, I look down at Dallas. If I draw power from his wound, my dark magic will become impossible to resist. But without it, I won't have enough magic left to unravel the spell that made Ratticus huge, or to help Cybil.

Xander puts his hand on my arm. "Are you sure you

want to do it that way?" His expression is anxious, as though he can see everything I'm thinking.

"It's the only way," I croak, pulling away from his hand.

I reach down and yank the knife out from Dallas's chest, placing one hand on his wound.

As Dallas's blood coats my hand, my mind fills with an oily blackness. The demon's magic rushes into me. Its power is immense, stronger than anything I've ever felt. Its stench fills my lungs and it feels like I'm touching Jeqabeel rather than Dallas.

The demon is forcing its magic into me.

I dimly remember Rebecca's vision of me standing next to the demon. In the vision, I was doing its bidding. Now I know why.

This is it. This is how it happens. The demon is possessing me. Its oily magic is oozing into me, using Dallas's dying body, his blood, as its conduit. It's filling every corner of my mind, taking over my thoughts. Turning me into its puppet.

Jeqabeel's mocking laughter sears into my mind.

The demon has won. It's sucking away my will, and I can't resist. It's taking control of me.

Then a sharp pain stabs into my shoulder. Blinding pain courses down my arm, and a petulant, shrill voice cuts through the demon's control. *"Hide me, stupid witch! HIDE ME!"*

My vision clears.

Ratticus is standing over me, screaming inside my head. Did he… did he *bite* me?

Clenching my fists, I force out the dark magic that's seething inside me. My magic gained power from Dallas's blood, even as the demon used its connection with Dallas to steal its way into my mind. Now, I use the dark magic to help me force back the demon's control, unwinding its tendrils from inside my brain. Jeqabeel screams with frustration as I wrench myself back from the demon's reach.

"Saffy." Xander's hand is on my arm, his face drawn with worry. "What's happening? Are you okay?"

I nod, panting with the effort of pushing out all the power I absorbed, expelling it in my efforts to make certain the demon's oily magic is fully out of my head. I feel violated. Filthy. My body is trembling and my throat burns with bile.

Ratticus looms over me again, as though he's going to take another chunk out of my shoulder, and Xander curses, swiping at him, forcing him back.

With the last bit of power I expel from my body, I reach up and unravel the strands of magic that are twisted over Ratticus's body, using the final scraps of my dark magic to work the unmaking spell and undo the chaotic and tangled mess of magic covering the quivering rat.

Ratticus squeals as he starts to shrink even faster than he grew, going down like a deflating balloon. I can't look at him at he shrinks. I can only stare at Dallas. Tendrils of the demon's magic are still wrapped around Dallas's body, the demon's trap still active.

I wipe my hand across my mouth, feeling sick. Jeqabeel came so close to possessing me. If Ratticus hadn't bitten me…

"Please help me," whimpers Jess. "She's bleeding."

Blinking, I twist back to Jess. She's still on her knees next to her mother. Xander moves over to her and crouches beside Cybil.

"Is she okay?" I drop to my knees at Cybil's other side. Her arms are bloody from scrapes, and there's more blood smeared on her face.

Even now, after the horror I just experienced, my

bloodlust surges and I can barely stop myself from reaching out to soak my hands with her blood.

"Mom hit the wall hard." Her face pale, Jess gives me a wild-eyed stare. "She might have some broken bones. Maybe something wrong with her lungs. She's not breathing properly."

"Heal her, Saff," says Xander. "Cast a spell to fix her. You can do that, can't you?" He strips off his jacket and rolls it up for a pillow, easing it under Cybil's head.

I clench my shaking hands and nod. The demon has never been inside Cybil, so it's safe to touch her. Still, I'm shaken. But there's no time to hesitate. If I don't heal her, she could die.

Putting my hand on the wound in Cybil's arm, I soak my fingers in her blood. The dark magic that jolts through me feels so intense, it overrides my fear at the demon somehow being able to worm itself inside me again. It also overrides my shame at the way I'm feeding from Cybil's pain.

Even as I reach inside me for a healing rune, using Cybil's own blood to power the dark magic needed to heal her, Cybil opens her eyes and coughs. Blood oozes from the corner of her mouth.

"It's okay, Mom." Jess grabs her mother's hand. "Saffy's going to heal you. You'll be fine."

I can feel Cybil's pain, how badly her injuries are hurting. But her cloudy eyes clear a little. "No," she croaks. "Don't heal me."

"What are you talking about?" Jess shakes her head. "Do it now, Saff. Quickly, before the demon gets here. I don't know how, but I can feel it coming. We don't have much time."

Xander glances up, his eyes troubled. "I can feel it too," he agrees.

"Listen to me." Cybil's breathing is labored, and I can tell it hurts her to talk, because with every sound she makes, my dark magic burns even stronger. "This is how it must be," she whispers. "I didn't want to admit why I didn't get to see you grow up, my darling daughter. But I knew all along. Only death could have kept me from you."

"No!" Jess bends closer to her, tears running down her face. "That's not true! It doesn't have to be that way. Saffy can heal you."

"I can save you." I take a breath, revelling in the feeling of my power building, at the way her blood is feeding it.

Cybil's clear gaze comes to rest on me. "Use my death to make you strong, Saffy. It's the only way you'll have enough magic to jump back so far. You won't make it otherwise."

I shake my head, trying to deny what she's saying. But there's something in her eyes that makes me hesitate.

"No." Jess's voice rises. "No, I won't let you—"

"There's no time to argue." Though Cybil's voice is weak, it doesn't falter. "You need my death to lock the demon inside the pentagram. That's all that matters."

"What if you used Dallas's death to get the power you need?" asks Xander, glancing to where Dallas's body lies behind us.

"I can't." My bile rises again at the suggestion. "The demon is using Dallas's body. When I tried to absorb his power, Jeqabeel almost took control of me."

Xander's eyes widen.

"You see?" Cybil coughs. "It has to be this way."

"Don't do this," begs Jess. "I can't lose you again."

"Don't you see, my darling? I get to save you. More than anything, I would have loved to have been there for you while you were growing up. But I look at the woman you've become, and I'm so proud. Please, let me do this for you."

Cybil eyes are so warm, my chest aches. Hot tears prick my eyes, even as the dark magic inside me rejoices in her suffering. My stomach churns at the confusing mix of elation and sorrow I'm feeling. I wish there was another way. Something else we could do. I wish I could tear the dark magic out of me and never use it again.

Xander is almost as pale as Jess, his expression drawn in anguish. He strokes the dying woman's hair, and he doesn't look up at me.

"Mom—" Jess's voice breaks.

"Trust me, Jess. I love you."

"I love you too. More than anything."

Cybil's gaze goes back to me. "Use my pain. Take my life. Save my daughter."

"You don't have to die," Jess wails. Xander puts his hand on her back, rubbing and murmuring soothing words.

Cybil's eyes close, and I can sense the life ebbing from her. My hands are coated in her blood, and her pain builds as her lungs shudder. "The demon..." Her whisper is so hoarse, it's all but inaudible. But I know what she's trying to say. Jeqabeel is almost here.

Then her head sags, and I can tell she's losing consciousness.

"I'm so sorry." Xander sounds stricken. "But she's right. You need to go before it's too late." He jumps up and rushes to the splintered mess of what used to be the book-case. Now back to normal size, Ratticus gives an indignant squeak as Xander fishes about in the rubble, disturbing the rat's hiding place.

Then Xander finds what he's looking for and pulls out the pentagramic antiprism.

I can't talk, my throat's too tight. I press my hands to the wound at Cybil's side. Though she's barely conscious, she lets out a tiny groan, and I want to snatch my hand away again, to stop myself from doing this. At the same time, I'm savoring her pain like a drunk savors wine.

Her suffering is making me strong.

"Stop," screams Jess. "You can't do this!"

"Jess listen to me." I speak quickly. "This is our one chance to change *everything*. We can make it so Jeqabeel never gets out of the bone. If we go back in time and stop the demon, the entire time line will be different and your mom might not need to die at all."

I have no idea if that's true, or if it's possible. But at least Jess isn't protesting anymore. She's staring at me, her eyes wide.

"Saffy's right." Xander presses the pentagramic antiprism into my hands, sounding a lot more convinced than I am. "Do this, and you can save the world, including your mom."

I swallow. He'd already gone out by the time Cybil told us about Atlantis. He has no idea how dangerous what we're doing really is.

"We have to go right now, though," I tell Jess, swallowing my doubts. "Otherwise it won't work, and your Mom's sacrifice will be for nothing."

Jess's tears drip onto her mother's hand as she raises it to her lips and kisses it. Her eyes are dark pools of grief, but her expression has turned resolute. She fixes me with a grim stare. "You promise we'll save her?"

"That's the plan, but you need to concentrate and get us to eighteen ninety four. You know exactly where and when we're going?"

Jess nods and closes her eyes. I stare at Xander, suddenly realizing what this could mean. If it goes wrong, if Jess can't get us to the right time, I may never see him again.

He's thinking the same thing, because he reaches for me, his expression desperate. His hands lock around my upper arms. "Wait," he says. "You know I love you, Saffy, right? I'll be waiting right here when you get back."

Cybil lets out one last tiny breath, then her heart stops beating. Her death fills me with an intense rush of power. Power I can't afford to waste.

"I love you too," I manage, but I'm already reaching for Jess's hand to pull her to her feet. I push my dark magic down the coven connection to her, clutching the heavy pentagram to my body with one hand and hanging onto Jess with the other.

Jess gasps as the magic hits her.

Xander vanishes.

Suddenly, I'm freezing and my vision is blurry. Jess grips my hand, her fingers digging into me. She's the only solid thing in a blurred, icy world, and a chill is seeping into my bones. The discordant sound I remember from before fills my ears, and Jess starts to glow.

The pentagramic antiprism is even heavier than when Xander gave it to me. In fact, it's growing heavier by the second, and my arm is already getting tired. I have it cradled to my stomach, terrified of dropping it. But it feels like it's trying to pull away from me. Like gravity isn't just pulling it down, but also sideways, out of my grip. And though the rest of my body feels like it's being blasted with ice, my stomach and hand are warm. The pentagram is heating up.

The blurriness around me turns into the soul-sucking *blackness* I remember from last time. The blackness extends toward me, reaching inside me. All that's holding it back is

Jess's golden glow. The light radiates out from her, making her look like an angel.

I turn to face her, wanting her glow to envelope me as much as possible. The front of my body is protected by it, but the skin on my back is crawling, like something horrible is behind me, lurking beyond Jess's glow.

The pentagram is getting hotter, and it's pulling so hard away from me now that I can barely hang onto it. The hand that's holding it is slicked with sweat, and it's in danger of slipping free.

Jess's face is pale, and she's saying something. Her expression is urgent, like whatever she's trying to say is vitally important. I can see her lips moving, but I can't hear anything but the discordant noise in my ears. I have no idea what she's trying to tell me.

Then I realize something that makes the chill in my bones even worse.

Jess's glow is starting to fade.

As her light dies, the blackness around us gets even deeper and colder, and I get the awful feeling that we're *inside* a demon. Somehow we've been swallowed whole.

A hollow emptiness grows inside me. Despair creeps through my body, weakening my limbs and turning my thoughts dark. Though I'm losing my grip on the penta- gramic antiprism, it's hard to care. What does it matter anyway when we're all doomed and nothing good can ever happen? We may as well give up—

Jess reaches out with her free hand and tears the penta- gramic antiprism out of my hand.

She lets it go.

It falls away from us and disappears.

I watch the pentagram, the one thing that could save us, vanish into blackness, and I feel sick.

Then the blackness around us turns into something

else. The blurriness is back, a sensation of movement instead of darkness. Although I can't make anything out, at least there's something there. Something beyond us.

Jess's glow is brightening. Could the pentagramic antiprism have been draining her magic?

The despair lifts from my mind, the feeling of doom disappearing. My brain is working again, and it's only now that normal thoughts are returning that I realize the blackness had stopped me from being able to think clearly.

Was that blackness the Nowhere? If so, I see why Jess is so afraid of it.

The pentagramic antiprism must have been interfering with her magic, so we were being sucked into the Nowhere. That has to be why she pushed it out of my hand.

I squeeze Jess's hand, wishing I could talk to her. Letting the pentagram go, and with it our one hope of changing the past and stopping her mother from dying, must have been the hardest decision of her life.

Without it, we have nothing. No plan. No way to fix anything.

The world around us solidifies.

It's cold, and rain is hitting me like needles. It's daytime, but the clouds above us are so thick and black, it's almost as dark as night. The wind is howling and in front of us is the crumbled remains of a large stone building.

I keep my grip on Jess's hand, trying to get my bearings. My body feels weak and my ears are still ringing.

Jess staggers. When I turn to her, I'm shocked by how pale and drawn she looks. And her eyes are black, just like when I use dark magic. But the fact I've infected her with a sign of something she hates is the least of our worries. The rain and wind are blasting her hair across her face, and defeat is written into every line of her body.

"I couldn't get us here with the pentagram." Her voice

is hoarse, and I can barely hear her over the roar of the wind.

"I know. I'm so sorry, Jess. But we made it here, so there's still hope." I'm trying to sound as upbeat as I can, but there's an empty pit where my stomach used to be. What can we possibly do to fix this?

Jess doesn't reply, so I tug on her hand, trying to snap her out of it. "Is this the Thomas Jefferson building?" I visited the building when I was a kid, learning about history. It's terrifying to see what was a solid stone building reduced to rubble.

Lightning flashes so brightly, it makes me jump, and thunder rolls loudly overhead. "Let's get out of the rain." I tug Jess to a corner of the building that still has some of the wall left, while she stumbles behind me like her feet are filled with lead.

"Look," she says when we get there, and I turn to where she's pointing.

Half hidden behind the rubble of the building is a circle of women holding hands. They're all wearing long dresses and dark cloaks, and the wind whips at the hoods covering their heads. There are several glass lanterns around them, glowing weakly. One of the women is holding an ancient grimoire in her hands, trying to keep the page open to a particular spell, but the wild weather is flapping the pages about. Dark magic pours from the book, and I shiver, even as my own dark magic tries to push me closer.

In the center of the circle looms the demon. It's just as big, and its hairy body and huge jackal head look just as ugly as they do in our time. Its broad, muscled shoulders are outlined every time lightning lights up the sky. The demon is snarling, its long snout curled back to expose its wicked fangs.

My dark magic rises more strongly inside me, burning to be set free. It's attracted by the demon, by its chaos. All the dark spells I absorbed are at the top of my consciousness. They're for causing death and destruction. Pain and suffering. Letting my dark magic free right now might create the future that the Veritas saw in her vision.

The witches look like they're chanting, but I can't hear what they're saying. If they're trying to bind the demon, it doesn't seem to be working.

As we reach the group, the demon lunges out with its wicked claws, slashing at the nearest witch. It's so fast, she doesn't even have time to move away. She screams as her torso blooms with blood, and drops to the ground. My dark magic surges even more strongly, fighting to be released.

The demon sniffs the air, then looks around as if trying to find the source of whatever it can smell.

Its gaze lands on us.

Chapter Twenty-Three

We stumble closer, my hand still wrapped tightly around Jess's arm, and the demon doesn't take its eyes off me. It sniffs the air again, and its snarl turns into a smirk. It can feel my dark magic. We come to a halt, and I crouch down over the injured witch. She's still alive, gasping for breath, but she's losing a lot of blood and I can feel her weakening. I could save her if I used my dark magic.

The other witches are casting worried looks at their fallen friend, and at me and Jess, but they're trying to keep their focus on the demon. This close, I can hear their chant. Jeqabeel is still inside their circle, so whatever they're doing must be holding it in place, but that could change in an instant if it manages to kill another of them.

Instead of healing the injured witch, I put my palms onto her wound, coating them in her blood.

Power floods through me me, lighting me up like a match thrown into gasoline. A blood-red haze covers everything around me, tainting my vision. I bring up runes onto my arms to control my magic, their power barely enough to contain the immense amount of power seething inside me.

The demon laughs.

Standing up, I take my place in the circle of witches who are keeping the demon pinned in place. Though their chanting is loud and firm, their power is weakening. I can feel them faltering. Soon the demon will kill another of them.

Jeqabeel's glowing, evil eyes meet mine. "Come to join me, dark witch?"

Remembering how it felt to have the demon worm its way into my brain and take control of me, I shudder.

But it extends its hand and its oily black magic oozes toward me. Suddenly all I can think of is the feel of the demon's immense, exhilarating power. If I agreed to its bargain, it would lend me that power. I could have anything. Do anything.

For a second, I teeter on the edge. I stare at the demon, lost in the glow of its eyes. Tempted beyond reason by the thought of bringing back all the people I've lost, and setting my world back to rights.

Then Jess is standing beside me, her chin lifted and her fists clenched. "Screw you, dog head." Jess's shout carries over the storm. "Crawl back into your kennel and *die.*"

She tugs me forward so we become part of the witch's circle, and begins chanting with the others, her voice joining with theirs. I can feel her magic mingling with theirs, strengthening it. Somehow she knows the words of the chant.

The woman holding the grimoire stops chanting and glares at me. Her face is lined and her hair pure gray. "You're a dark witch." Her voice is accusing and her eyes blaze with a mixture of fear, hate, and fury.

"I am." I yell the words so all the witches can hear. "But I'm on your side."

Another witch turns her head to me. Her eyes are pure white. She's a Veritas. White strands of magic twist from her to each woman in turn, all the way around the circle, including Jess and me.

"You help us, instead of the demon?" demands the witch with the grimoire.

"Jeqabeel has killed people I love." I meet her glare with an impatient shake of my head. "Why haven't you bound it yet? If Jeqabeel gets loose, it'll kill you all."

"We can't contain it." She motions to a the shards of what looks like a shattered pot on the ground. "It broke our receptacle."

"What about the bone?"

She frowns. "Bone?"

"Jeqabeel will consume any vessel that contains it." I recite the words from Arabella Lightfoot's book. "That's why you need to put its essence inside its own bone. It'll eventually get out, but it'll take over a hundred years." I say the words bitterly, knowing my actions will cause events to happen just as I experienced them. I'm condemning Jess's mother to death, along with my own parents, Sylvia, Theresa, and everyone else the demon has killed.

Putting the demon's essence in its own bone means nothing will change. But what choice do I have? We can't let it go free in this time either.

"How do we get the demon's bone?" she asks.

"Saff," says Jess urgently. "We don't have much time. I don't know if you can feel it, but we're being pulled back to the present day. Mom never got a chance to teach me how to resist the pull, and I won't be able to hold us here much longer."

The knot in my stomach hardens. If we get pulled back

to our present day before the demon is bound, who knows what chaos it'll cause? We could get back to an America that's completely destroyed. Wiped off the face off the earth, like Atlantas.

I lift my hands, pulling up every bit of magic I have inside me. Piles of rubble surround us, which gives me lots of ammunition to work with, but I've made the mistake of underestimating the demon before.

When I let my earth magic spread into the rocks and debris around me, then motion them up, it looks and feels like the entire ground rises. Like our small circle of witches is an island, and an enormous tidal wave of rock is being pulled over our heads.

The witches gasp, their voices stumbling over the chant that's holding Jeqabeel contained. The demon swipes forward, using their momentary distraction to break free, but the Veritas's glowing white magic brightens, feeding the other witches the right words to push the demon back into place.

Holding the rocks in place, I focus on where I'm going to throw them.

I drag in a breath, letting the magic build.

Then I slam the sea of rock into the demon, using my frustration and rage to force it down *hard*. I pound the demon's body into pieces, grinding all its limbs into dust, except for its right leg. That's the leg I'm keeping whole.

A giant cloud of dust billows out as the rocks rain down. The noise is deafening. The roar of the rocks landing is as loud as an avalanche, so loud that the demon's howls of pain and fury are barely audible over it.

I keep hold of the rocks, bringing them back up and down again, pounding the demon over and over. Breaking its bones and pulverising its flesh.

As the rocks crack and shatter, so does the demon. I

feel it happen. Last time I tried to crush the demon with rock, it survived. But it's weaker in this time because it hasn't collected all the blood and suffering that's made it so strong in our present. And I'm stronger than I used to be.

It can't survive the onslaught of rock.

I'm killing it, grinding both rock and demon into dust.

I hack and cough as the dust fills my lungs, and blink the blinding grime out of my eyes. Around me, the witches do the same. The circle has broken down, the witches no longer chanting. They can't chant with their lungs full of rock dust.

My earth magic runs out and I let the fragments of rock that remain fall to the ground. The demon is crushed, but one leg remains. One black, hairy leg is still untouched. It's surrounded by black blood and gore, but the demon's entire leg bone is intact.

An oily black substance coils up from it, forming a black shadow above it. The demon's physical form is escaping to seek a hiding place like it did when it possessed Xander. The oily black smoke moves toward one of the witches.

If it reaches her, we've lost.

"Keep chanting," I scream at the witches.

They're still coughing and spluttering, but they stare at me wide-eyed for a moment, then obey. The words come out hoarse and croaky, from throats that are still filled with dust, but the oily demon-essence recoils, shrinking away from the woman.

"Saffy," yells Jess. "It's pulling us, and I can't stop it." If her face wasn't already wet with rain, I'm sure it would be slicked with sweat. She looks like she's suffering, like she's using every bit of strength she has to keep us in this time.

"Hang on, Jess! I need another minute."

I whirl to the witch holding the grimoire and put both

my blood-streaked hands on the book. She tries to yank it away, her eyes narrowed with suspicion, even as she still chants with the others. But I've already called up the Binde Magick spell, and my hands sink right into the grimoires pages. I drag every dark spell out of the book and feel my power swell, the heat and fury of it enough to burn.

"What are you doing?" gasps the witch, disgust and horror on her face. "You've taken the spell we need!"

But the spell is inside me now. A binding spell that will encase the demon. All I need is the power to wield it.

Stepping to the injured witch on the ground, I press my hands to her wound once more, sucking out her life force. I take her magic, as I once watched the Unseen do to a dying witch. It horrified and repulsed me then. Now, all I can feel is a fierce joy as the witch's power floods into me.

Straightening, I let the words of the spell write themselves not just on my arms, but on my entire body. They burn themselves into my face and neck, across my chest, down my legs. My mouth opens and the words speak themselves, searing themselves into my throat and tongue as they go, and tumbling from my lips. The words are so hot, they glow as they come out of me. They spark and smoke, and ignite the air in front of me.

The spell hits Jeqabeel's essence, pushing it into the demon's leg.

At the same time, I use my animal magic to strip the bone clean, burning the flesh and muscle so it falls off the bone and scatters into ash. With no meat to hold them together, the bones fall apart.

I pour Jeqabeel's essence into its bone, using all my stolen power to force in every last bit of the black, oily smoke.

When it's done, the bone lies on the ground with nothing to show it's not an ordinary object.

The demon is bound. Jeqabeel will remain in that bone for more than a hundred years, until it manages to possess Uncle Ray and make him kill my parents.

The injured witch is dead at my feet. Her life was the price.

The other witches are staring at me, a mix of awe and horror on their faces. I can tell they're wondering whether to thank me or condemn me. But my magic is almost completely drained now, and suddenly I'm so exhausted it's hard to care what they think. I want to close my eyes and sleep for a thousand years.

As the women all step warily closer, my gaze goes to one I hadn't seen properly until now. I do a double take. She looks just like Sylvia, my father's cousin.

"Sylvia?" I ask, before I notice that her hair is a darker brown, and she has a bigger nose than Sylvia in my time.

"My name is Arabella Lightfoot," says the witch.

I gape at her. "*You* wrote that book?"

She frowns. "What book?"

"I absorbed a book that contained the Binde Magick spell. It's only thanks to that book that I was able to absorb all the other grimoires."

Arabella nods. "I was working on such a spell, but I stopped as soon as I realised how dangerous it would be." She frowns at me. I guess she thinks I'm a walking cautionary tale. A living warning about the dangers of absorbing too much magic.

"You need to work on it again," I tell her. "Thanks to your book, I learned to control my animal and earth magic. It saved Xander and the Blood Council. It got Jess and me here to contain Jeqabeel."

"I don't think that spell is a good idea," says Arabella. "It would give witches too much power. It could do more harm than good." She looks at Jeqabeel's bone, obviously torn. "But if it's the only reason you'll be able to bind the demon—" Her cautious gaze goes back to me, weighing and assessing me. She looks so much like Sylvia it makes me want to grab her and give her a big hug. Probably not the reaction she's expecting.

"Promise me you'll write that book. Bind it to me, to my blood, and include these spells—" I rattle off the ones that were useful to me. "Keep it in your family, tell them to keep it close."

"Saffy, we need to go." Jess grabs my hand, squeezing it tight. "Or I'll get pulled back without you."

"I don't have any magic left to give you," I whisper.

"I don't think I'll need it. The magic wants us back in our own time, and it's going to draw us back..."

The words aren't even out of her mouth before the whole world blurs.

The jump back to our own time seems quicker, but that's probably because I'm not holding a pentagramic antiprism that's trying to drag us into the Nowhere, and my brain is buzzing, turning over everything that happened, trying to figure out what I could have done differently. Is there anything I could have done that might have changed things for the better?

When the world solidifies around us, we're back in the rubble of the Unseen's house.

The demon is standing in front of us, huge, black, and hairy, with its eyes glowing. It's grasping Xander's neck in one clawed hand. Xander can't speak. His hands grip the demon's claws, trying to pull them away from his throat.

"Xander," I gasp, tugging my hand free of Jess's.

With his throat constricted, Xander can't answer. But his expression is full of terror.

When I take a step toward him, I see the demon's grip

tighten around Xander's throat. Heart hammering, I freeze.

"Let him go!" I yell.

The demon throws back its head to give a rumbling laugh. "Or what?" it asks.

"Or I'll kill you." It's the only thing I can think of to say, but it's an empty threat. I can feel the demon's power, far greater than back in eighteen hundred and ninety four. In this time, it's killed hundreds of people. Its bathed in a river of blood, and commands the power of the Blood Council as well as its own immense power.

In this time, I may as well be a bug for all the harm I could do it. Even if my tank weren't empty and I had some power left, I'd still be no threat to it.

The demon's lips curl back from its fangs and it looks like it's smiling.

"Come on, little witch," it mocks. "Do your worst."

Then it cuts Xander's throat.

Chapter Twenty-Four

Jess screams.

My heart stops. My mouth opens, but I can't make a sound.

Blood runs from Xander's throat. His hands drop and his head sags. His skin goes white, and his lips turn blue.

I can sense his life force draining away.

His lungs gurgle as they fill with blood. Then I feel him die.

My entire body flushes icy cold, and I can't draw in a breath. The shock is as sudden as a slap. I stagger, my legs too weak to support my weight.

The demon drops Xander and he lands heavily, crumpling into a lifeless pile.

Xander's dead. I can't believe it, but I felt it happen. I could tell the instant his life force faded.

I realize I'm making a sound, an awful keening noise, as I stumble toward his body. The demon steps forward, into my path. It grabs me by one shoulder, its claws closing roughly, cutting into me. When I hear another

sobbing scream, I realize it's caught Jess with its other claw.

It holds us both, one in each hand. Its eyes glow and its lips peel back from its teeth. It stinks anyway, but its breath is so revolting it makes me gag. The stench is so shocking, it kickstarts my brain so I can think again.

Though Xander's dead, I must still be alive to be smelling something that putrid. I have to get away from the demon. I have to get *Jess* away from it.

Turning, I see she's struggling against its grip, but it's holding her easily. Blood runs down her clothes from where its claws are digging into her, and she's cursing it, calling it every name under the sun.

For a moment I wonder why she doesn't time travel to get away from it. But I guess with it holding her, she'd only take it with her.

Jeqabeel ignores Jess, focusing on me instead. "The Veritas showed me her visions," it growls. "I've seen the future. I know you join with me and use your power to help me."

"Never!" I shout the word into its face, splattering its snout with my spittle. Not that it seems to notice or care.

"Your dark magic is getting stronger," it says. "I feel your lust for power. You want the power only I can give you. Your longing for it will soon consume you."

The demon isn't wrong. Though my heart is broken, part of me only cares about the power I can wield. The dark magic is corrupting me, and my bloodlust is over-riding my decency and humanity. I don't know how much longer I can fight it.

Jeqabeel chuckles. "Your lover is dead. Now you can watch me consume the magic from the last friend you have left in the world. Once that's done, I will be all you have left."

I clench my jaw. "Go to hell." I hiss the words from between my teeth.

"The vision must come true. Accept my rule and I will give you the power to bring them back from the dead, if you still wish it." He tightens his grip on Jess, making her scream with pain. "Accept my rule and I will allow you to consume part of your friend's magic. You have tasted her power before. Now claim it for your own."

I have tasted Jess's power, and even now, with Jess crying out in agony beside me, I'm tempted to accept, so I can get more of it.

But I know what will happen. After the demon kills Jess, it'll chain me to it, forcing me to do such unspeakable things with my dark magic that there'll be nothing left of me. It'll use me up and throw me away.

Problem is, I can't fight it.

Nothing I do can hurt the demon. It's invulnerable here, and I don't know how to return it to its own dimension. The only other place I've ever been, besides this dimension is—

I wriggle in its grip, making its claws dig deeper, ripping more of my skin.

My blood flows thickly, soaking my T-shirt and dripping onto my jeans. My regular animal and earth magic is a lot weaker than my dark magic, but I don't need much of it.

"Jess," I hiss, pushing what little I have left of my magic through our coven link. "Take us to the Nowhere."

Jess stares at me, still fighting to get out of the demon's grip. Her eyes widen and understanding flicks across her face.

Then the world disappears.

The demon's claws loosen from my shoulder, and I reach across its body, grabbing frantically for Jess. I have no idea what would happen to me if I got disconnected from Jess while time travelling, and I don't want to find out. I latch onto her hand and hang on tight.

Jess is already glowing, her magic filling her with a warm golden aura. The demon hugs her to its hairy chest, its long arms wrapped around her like a lover's embrace.

The discordant sound in my ears means I can't hear anything, but the demon's snout is open, and with my hand gripping Jess's, my shoulder is touching its side, so I can feel Jeqabeel's torso vibrating. It's the weirdest feeling, like the demon is purring. More likely, it's snarling.

My feelings of hopelessness and dread get stronger, but the difference is that this time, I'm expecting to feel that way. It's this place, wherever it is, that's filling me with despair. And just knowing that helps me to fight it. Even when the feeling grows and gets stronger.

The discordant sound fades, and now I can hear the demon snarling. It's still dark, pitch black, but I think we've arrived. There's something solid under my feet.

This place seems to be *made* of despair. No light can survive here. No hope, except for Jess's golden glow.

It's the Nowhere.

"Take us back," snarls Jeqabeel. "Now!"

Jess gasps with pain and I assume the demon is digging its claws harder into her. But I can hear other noises now too, and I'm straining my eyes into the blackness trying to see what horrors might be lurking in the dark.

Instinctively I reach inside for my magic. It's not there.

My magic isn't just used up. It's *gone*. Completely dead. It feels like when the Blood Council bound it so I couldn't even feel it anymore.

Then I realize why.

There's nothing here resembling soil or rock, or any natural material from Earth. Whatever I'm standing on, my magic doesn't recognize it as real ground. My earth magic has nothing to draw on.

The noises around us sound like they're coming from living things. I can hear what sounds like feet shuffling. Mouths slurping. The gnashing of teeth. The scrape of claws on whatever it is that I'm standing on. But my animal magic is dead too.

Whatever the creatures are that are moving around us, they're not animals.

They're demons.

I can tell they're demons, because I can feel their dark power. And past the edges of the glow cast by Jess's aura, I sense seething movement. A lot of movement.

There has to be dozens of demons out there. Maybe hundreds. Hell, there could be *millions* of them for all we know. We're blind, surrounded by a demon army.

Jess is the only bright thing in the darkness. She's a glowing ember in a black wasteland of despair.

Something gets close enough to her that her light extends out to it. I can see a hint of it now, in the glow. A horrible, slimy, deformed creature with a misshapen head and octopus limbs. Jess's glow fades a little as the creature sucks down her magic.

It's stealing her glow. Taking her power.

"No! Get back!" I yank my small knife from my jeans pocket and lurch toward it, though I feel like a mosquito buzzing at dragon. If the demon takes Jess's magic, we'll be stuck here. We'll die in darkness, devoured by demons.

Jeqabeel swipes at the demon, slicing through it with the claws on one hand. It keeps its other hand on Jess, gripping her wrist, clearly worried she'll jump away and leave it here.

As Jeqabeel drags Jess forward, another demon darts

in. There are too many of them. If we stay here, they'll steal all her power.

With a furious roar, Jeqabeel claws the demon, cutting it in two. It's too dark to see blood spurt, but something wet and disgusting splatters my face.

Demon blood.

The dark magic inside me surges in response. The demon blood has power.

But it's not like human blood. It feels oily and filthy. It stinks of rot and decay. Of evil and fear.

But it has power. And if we don't get out of here, we'll die.

Jeqabeel's still holding tight to Jess, and the demons surrounding us are being drawn to her. They're ignoring me. I don't have any magic here, in this place, and at least until Jess's magic is gone, her golden glow is all they're focused on.

"Take us back," the demon commands, shaking her. "Do it now, before they bleed you dry."

"Go to hell," she snaps. But Jeqabeel is right, Jess's glow is fading fast. It's half of what it was when we arrived. Soon she won't be able to get us back at all.

Another demon launches itself at Jess. In the faint glow she emits, I see it's large and mostly hairless, with wrinkled, sagging skin. Giant whiskers protrude from the shapeless lump that must be its face, and its mouth—snout—is drawn back into a snarl that shows off three rows of sharp, pointed fangs.

Jeqabeel swipes one long arm at the creature and it falls dead at the demon's feet. But more are already pressing forward, lunging at Jess.

Jeqabeel shakes her again. "If you don't take us back now, I'll tear your arms off and feed them to these *creatures*." He spits the last word out, like they're too far below him to be called demons.

"Kill me, and you'll be stuck here forever."

As Jeqabeel strikes at more demons, dragging Jess behind it, I stumble to one of the wounded monsters on the ground. A black, oily substance is oozing out of the demon.

Bracing myself, I sink my hands into the demon's blood. The shock of it vibrates up my body. Its power oozes into me like disgusting slime. It makes me feel unbearably dirty, like I want to peel my skin right off to get rid of it.

But I grit my teeth and drag the demon's power into my body. I let it fill me up, let it change and warp my own magic.

It distorts my power.

It corrupts it.

But it's strong, and right now, that's all that counts. Slimy and horrible as the demon power is, if I can save Jess, it'll be worth it.

Another demon falls, almost sliced in half by Jeqabeel's powerful claws, and I crawl to that one next. When I sink my hands into its wound, my power feeds on its suffering, growing strong. Growing dark.

I can feel myself mutating. Changing. Becoming even darker than I already was.

The thought horrifies me, even as my new power surges through my veins.

I yank my hands away from the demon and turn to where Jeqabeel is crouched over Jess's prone body, fighting off the pack. Jeqabeel still has a hand on Jess, but she's not moving, and her power has dimmed. She's wounded, and almost drained.

She's dying.

There are too many demons for Jeqabeel to hold them off much longer. Until Jess dies, they'll keep coming. And Jeqabeel is wounded. The demon seems weaker than before, its body slashed open in several places.

It's growing weak, and I feel strong.

The demon blood might be disgusting, but it's filled my depleted energy reserves, and it's powering my dark magic. I may not have earth magic or animal magic in this place, but I no longer need it.

Bringing up all the demon magic inside me, I launch myself at Jeqabeel.

Black strands of magic ooze from my skin, wrapping themselves around the hand that's holding onto Jess. I push the magic into the demon's skin, slicing through its flesh as though it were butter.

Jeqabeel roars with agony, and I feel my lips pull up into a humorless smile.

"I told you I'd kill you," I say out loud.

Then I tighten the demon magic like a tourniquet, and with one quick twist I cut off Jeqabeel's arm.

Grabbing Jess, I yank her away from the demon. Her power is all but extinguished, her glow so dim it's barely there. Her eyes are open, but I don't think she can see me, or that she knows what's happening. She's too weak to register anything.

Roaring, the demon lunges at me, its eyes filled with rage. It sweeps one clawed hand down and I hunch over Jess, protecting her with my body as I pour my demon magic into her.

Her eyes flick open as Jeqabeel's claws rake my back, flaying my skin open. Pain sears through me, hot and unbearable. This is it for me, but at least my death will be quick.

"Go!" I scream at Jess, the words barely formed

through my agony. "Jump back to our time." At least one of us will survive.

Turning to face Jeqabeel, I brace my legs and hold up both shaking hands, determined to fend off the demon while she jumps. I'm going to make sure she gets to live. It's the least I can do.

I feel her surge to her feet behind me, and instead of disappearing instantly, she throws her arms around my waist. Jeqabeel rushes at me, claws raised to strike a killing blow.

Then everything blurs.

Chapter Twenty-Five

The discordant sound fills my ears, and pain throbs through my whole body. My back is hot and sticky with blood, and Jess is pressed against my wound, either applying pressure to it or making it worse, it's hard to tell.

I feel changed. Less human than I was before. I wonder if my blood is black like the demons I stole power from.

Jess should have left me behind, in the Nowhere.

Even if she manages to get us back to our own time, I'm not sure I want to go. With Xander gone, I don't know if I even have the will to live anymore. I've lost so many people I love, I can't bear that I've lost Xander too.

The world solidifies around us.

We're back, and what's left of the Unseen's living room is a splintered mess.

Xander's body is lying on the floor.

As soon as Jess lets me go, I sink to my knees beside him. It seems like he died hours ago, like he should be cold by now, but his skin is still warm. Jess has brought us back to just after we left, so he must have only just died.

But he's really dead. His pulse is still. His heart is no longer beating, and blood has stopped flowing from the gaping wound in his neck.

"Saffy?" Jess puts her hand on my arm. "Are you…?" Her voice breaks, and even though I know what she's asking, I can't answer out loud. I'm as far from okay as it's possible to get.

Instead I ask, "You're okay?" She looks drawn and her skin is gray, but at least she's alive.

She draws in a shuddering breath. "Your veins, Saffy."

I glance up at her, frowning. Then I look down at my hands. My veins are black. They look a little like the roots of a tree, but much uglier.

"My veins are filled with demon magic." My voice comes out flat. I think I'm out of shock, out of tears. My heart barely feels like it's beating. I feel as dead inside as Xander.

"I know," she says. "I felt it."

I close my eyes, feeling the power that's coursing through me. I barely used any of it up, and it's far stronger than my old magic. It might be filthy and evil, but… An idea whispers in my head, and my heart quickens. Could I…?

Flicking my eyes open, I put my hands on Xander. Bringing up a healing rune on my arm, I fill it with demon magic.

Then I pour the magic into Xander.

Xander's neck is gaping open, but as I fill him with magic, his skin knits together. The wound seals, and his face starts to look less waxy. Hope rushes through me and I drag more of the demon magic out, forcing it into Xander.

His chest moves. He drags in a gurgling breath. Then he takes another, clearer breath. His eyes flicker slowly open.

My heart is singing and all I want to do is throw my arms around him.

And then he looks at me with fear and confusion in his eyes.

For a second, I'm frozen. Then I remember. I'm hideous. I pull away, stumbling back. I can see myself reflected in his eyes, my skin only just covering a pulsing, living spider's web of black veins. I look like the monster I am. I've become one of *them*. I'm just like Jeqabeel.

Demonic. Corrupted. Evil.

I don't want Xander to see me like this.

"Saffy?" He sits up slowly, bringing one hand up to rub his neck. His throat is still covered with blood, and he gets it all over his hand, but doesn't seem to notice. Instead, he's staring at me. I back up, shaking my head. All my veins are black, and though I turn my face away, I can't hide my arms and hands.

"I… I'm sorry." My throat is so tight I can barely get the words out. "It was the only way I could…" My voice breaks as he scrambles to his feet. "Please don't come any closer, Xander. You don't know what I am now."

"What you are?" He walks carefully toward me, and with the wall behind me I can't back up any further. "You look a little weird, but I'm just grateful we're both alive." Then he wraps his arms around me in a crushing hug.

His embrace doesn't hurt, because somehow the gaping wounds in my back must have healed on their own, without me even being aware of it. But my muscles are too stiff to hug Xander back. "Jess took us to the Nowhere," I tell him. "We left Jeqabeel there, but I had to absorb demon power. I *used* it."

"I remember Jeqabeel cutting my throat," he whispers. "You healed me."

"Yes, but the demon power changed me." He still doesn't

seem to get it, so as awful as it is, I'm determined to lay it out for him. "I felt the demon's essence corrupting my magic. Corrupting *me*. I have demon magic inside me now." His arms are still around me, and I ease myself free and step back so he can get a good look at me. I have no doubt the veins in my face are just as black and ugly as the ones on my arms and hands. "See?" I demand. "I might be part demon."

Xander studies me. "Okay, so it's not my favorite look," he admits. "But you're still you. And I love you, Saff. Nothing can ever change that."

"You got us out of the Nowhere," says Jess from behind me. "If you hadn't absorbed demon magic, we would have died there." When I look back at her, she's standing with her arms folded and her chin lifted. "So what if you're a little veiny now? As far as I'm concerned, it's practically a badge of honor."

Xander pulls me into another hug, and this time I let myself relax in his arms. When he tightens them around me it feels like heaven. I didn't believe I'd ever get to experience one of his hugs again.

"So you left Jeqabeel in the Nowhere." His voice rumbles in my ear. "You think it'll stay there?"

"I don't know." I let out a deep sigh, feeling better with every breath. "I hope so."

"*Is it safe now?*" I can't see Ratticus, but I can hear his voice in my head. No doubt he's wedged himself into a rat-sized hiding place somewhere.

"What happens now?" Jess asks, before I can say anything. "The demon is gone, and Dallas is dead. You think things will go back to normal?"

"I don't know. But I hope the Veritas and Magnus are still alive. If so, I guess they'll put together another Blood Council, and fix things as much as they can."

"Jeqabeel killed people on live television," Xander points out. "Unless they can wipe people's memories, there's no way to fix that."

"They'll probably find a way," I say. But he's right. A lot of people have died, and there's no way even the most powerful witches can fix that. Life is sure to be very different now, no matter what they do.

And they probably won't be happy to have a black-veined, part-demon witch walking around, reminding people that magic and demons are real.

Reaching deep inside me, I find a spell from one of the dark magic grimoires. It's a way for a witch to use animal magic to change their appearance. I use the demon magic to power it, letting the spell flow over my body, turning my black veins and eyes back to their normal colour. Underneath the magic, the black is still there. But Xander smiles at me.

"See?" he says. "You were worried about nothing. You're not corrupted and you're definitely not evil. Whatever turned your veins dark, it's already worn off."

I glance at Jess who raises her eyebrows at me. She's not so easily convinced, but I know she'll keep my secret. If dark magic is forbidden, demon magic will definitely mark me for some kind of horrific witch death. But hopefully the Blood Council will never find out about it.

"*I know what you are.*" Ratticus has scuttled out of hiding, and his whiskers quiver as he sniffs me. "*I can smell the demon power inside you.*"

I don't bother to answer. Nobody else can hear him talking, so he's not exactly going to tell, is he?

Besides, the power that's now inside me is insanely strong. That's got to come in handy, right?

Maybe the demon power will eat me alive. Perhaps it'll

consume me and turn me into a monster. Or maybe I'm worried about nothing, and I'll be able to control it.

Guess I'll find out eventually.

Epilogue

"Which episode are you watching?" asks Jess, calling through from the kitchen.

"The one about the fire ants," I call back.

"Oooh, I love that one."

"Shhh!" says Rebecca from where she's curled up on a bean bag. "I haven't seen this one, even if you two have." She's wearing ripped jeans and a Flaming Buttholes T-shirt, and she's glued to the screen. Earlier today, without asking anyone's permission, she dissolved every statue spell to turn all the statues in the council chambers back into witches. She's becoming quite the rebel. I'm kinda proud of her.

Jess comes into the room with a huge bowl of popcorn and sits on the big squishy chair next to the sofa that Xander and I are lounging on. I'm lying with my head on his legs, and he's brushing the hair back from my face. It feels wonderful.

Though I've made myself look normal, I'm still part

demon. I still have more power than any normal witch. I'm still *corrupted*.

But right now it's pretty hard to care. Not with Xander's thigh pressing against my cheek and his fingers gently stroking the side of my face.

Jess passes over the popcorn and I take a handful. Xander pops a couple of pieces into his mouth, and passes it over to Rebecca.

"Don't hog the popcorn," Ratticus grumbles. He's sitting on the bean bag next to Rebecca, and he's just finished stuffing the last of his popcorn into his mouth. His furry belly is already distended, but she fills his bowl with more anyway.

"This is the life, demon-veins," says Ratticus, as he pops another piece into his mouth.

I'm trying not to let on how annoying his new nickname for me is, because if he finds out, he'll use it even more. I'm constantly tempted to take him to Morgan's place and leave him there, but for some weird reason I think I might miss the irritating little guy. Maybe the demon magic has turned me into a masochist.

Besides, Rebecca likes him, and I don't want to upset her. She's already been through enough. She's started hanging out with us, staying over whenever I can convince Magnus that it's better for a thirteen-year-old girl to hang out with other people, rather than at the Council Chambers on her own.

On the television, MacGyver is talking to someone, his brown eighties jacket and mullet filling the screen. It's a great episode, but I've seen it before, and right now is a slow part. I'm content to just drift off into my own thoughts of how amazing it is to be able to finally have a night on the couch with Xander, without being afraid for our lives.

He strokes his hand over my back and I turn a little to give him better access. When he scratches lightly at the skin under my shoulder blades that always seems to be a little itchy, it makes me want to purr.

"How's your mom?" Jess asks Xander.

"She's much better." He shoots her a smile. "Coming home from hospital in a couple of days."

"That's great news." Jess smiles back.

Xander's mother was lucky. I'm still not sure why the demon didn't kill her, but maybe it thought she could still be useful. Plenty of people weren't as lucky, but the burials and memorial services are all done now, and for most people, life seems to be slowly returning to normal.

"Did you see your father today?" I ask Jess.

She nods. "He's got a good group of people around him on the council now." Her gaze flicks to Rebecca where she's lounging on the bean bag.

"Including you?" I ask.

"Including me, yes."

"Are you definitely going to visit Chicago?"

She nods. "The time witch there has agreed to train me."

I still don't quite understand why that didn't happen in the first place. Why Magnus decided to bind Jess's powers instead of helping her to control them is beyond me.

"He was grieving," says Jess, as though I'd asked the question aloud. "He's talked to me about it. Apologised."

"Good for him." I can't imagine Magnus apologizing for anything, but I guess he must have changed. Becoming enslaved to Jeqabeel was probably a humbling experience for him. I've been keeping my distance from him, and the rest of the council, so I couldn't say for sure.

"What about the Foxy Bottoms?" asks Xander.

Jess grins. "The Flaming Buttholes are coming with

me. They think the scene in Chicago will be great for the band, and we've already got a whole lot of gigs lined up there. It's going to be fun."

She sounds happy. Picking up the pieces after the demon's reign of terror hasn't been easy for anyone, but it seems like life is coming together for Jess.

Who knows, maybe she and Mikey will finally admit they have feelings for each other. I hope so, but either way, I'm happy for her.

"We'll miss you," I say. "So post lots of photos, okay?"

She gives a casual shrug. "You know what they say. What happens in Chicago, stays in Chicago."

"That's not a thing." I screw my face up. "Come on. I'm going to miss seeing you play live."

"Maybe it's time you went back to work," she points out. "You haven't had any big stone walls to build for ages."

I look over at the paint tins that have been piled up in the corner of my living room, gathering dust. "There's going to be plenty of work now that the rebuilding of the city's started," I admit. "But I think I'm going to finally finish the house renovations first. It's about time I got the last coat of paint on these walls, don't you think?"

I could probably use my new power to finish the work instantly. One spell and it could all be done. But I've done so much of it through hard, pain-staking labor that the thought of finishing it with magic doesn't appeal. I want to roll that last coat on the walls by hand, then be able to step back and admire the results of my hard work.

Call me old fashioned, but the fact that I have no urge to use magic to finish it is comforting. It means there might still be hope for me.

"Speaking of work, I've been assigned my first case at work that isn't demon-related," says Xander. "Just a regular murder. A woman stabbed, and I'm almost certain her husband did it."

"That's great," I say without thinking.

Jess laughs. "Lovely, I'm sure." She shakes her head at me. "Saffy, I think you need to take a vacation. Hawaii, or something. No corpses, no demons, no magic. Just palm trees and cocktails."

"That sounds nice."

I must sound a little wistful, because Xander smiles down at me. "Hawaii?" he says. "Sounds like a great idea."

I grin up at him. "Would they even give you the time off work right now?"

"Maybe not," he admits. "There were a lot of detectives who didn't survive the demon's destruction of the city. But I have something else you might like." He pulls a little square jewellery case out of his back pocket. My heart starts beating a little faster. Surely he's not…?

I sit up carefully, not taking my eyes off the little box. Xander hands it to me. "Saffy," he says, his expression serious. "This is for you."

I take the box from him, staring down at it. I don't know if I'm ready for marriage just yet. I mean, I love Xander, I don't want anyone else. But, really…? During MacGyver?

Unable to stop myself, I flip the box open.

Inside, there's no ring. I let out a relieved breath. But there *is* a folded-up piece of paper. I frown at Xander. "What's this?"

"Just open it." He nods at the paper, and I can see he's trying to suppress a grin.

I unfold the page, and look down at the printed receipt. It's a voucher. For Netflix. In my name. "You got me a Netflix account?"

"I figured you might want to stay in with me and watch

movies more often. And you know that nobody loves the eighties more than I do, but maybe we could try watching something that was made a little more recently."

A grin spreads across my face and a surge of warmth fills my chest. The feeling is stronger and better than any magic could ever be. Still, I force the smile from my face and make my expression stern.

"Are you just asking me to watch Netflix with you because you know I can bring you back to life if something bad happens?" I demand.

"Of course," he agrees just as seriously. "You're my Get Out Of Jail Free card. Can't blame me for wanting to keep you around."

"In that case, of course we can watch Netflix together." I let my grin take over my face, unable to hide my happiness for a second longer.

Xander leans back in the couch and holds out his arms for me so I can snuggle into his warmth. I have no idea how I'm going to actually get Netflix to work on my father's magical eighties-only television, but dammit, I'm gonna try.

"*I don't want to watch anything scary,*" grumbles Ratticus. "*Can't we get Animal Planet?*"

"I'm looking forward to Netflix," I say.

Xander tightens his arms around me. "Me too," he murmurs in my ear.

"Everything's going to work out, right?" I ask. "This is our happy ending?"

"Absolutely," he says with a smile.

And despite the demon blood in my veins, I can't help but believe him.

Authors' Note

Thank you for reading The Danger With Demons!

We're so happy you came along with us on this journey, and we're extremely relieved that Saffy and the others are safe, for now at least.

This is the first series we've worked on together and we've had a blast! Other books we've written as individuals are listed on the next page. You can also stalk us at www.trudijayewrites.com and www.taniahutley.com

Thanks once more for your wonderful support. We couldn't do this without you.

Tania and Trudi.

Also by Tania and Trudi

By Trudi Jaye

Dragon Rising Urban Fantasy Series

Dark Carnival Series

Firecaller Urban Fantasy Series

By Tania Hutley

Skin Hunter Science Fiction Series